ENLIGHTENED

THE ORACLE CHRONICLES
BOOK 2

BY

MONI BOYCE

LOVE SNACKS PUBLISHING

Love Snacks Publishing, LLC

Enlightened: The Oracle Chronicles © 2019 Shaquana M. Boyce

www.lovesnackspublishing.com

First Edition
ISBN: 978-1-7333937-0-6

Book cover design by: Mallory Rock of Rock Solid Book Design

ENLIGHTENED

CHAPTER 1

Willow

"YOU'RE BEAUTIFUL." His voice slithered over her skin like a multitude of snakes. The terror that engulfed her felt like she was caught in a vipers' nest, waiting for the venomous animals to spring and attack at any moment. She shuddered. Peering at her reflection in the mirror, she took in the red, silk, strapless dress that clung to her curves and brushed the floor. Killian stood behind her. His breath raised the hairs on the back of her neck and her skin became pebbled with gooseflesh.

He was clad in a tuxedo. She wondered about the special occasion that had them dressed in formal wear. Better yet, maybe she didn't want to know.

She was afraid to speak, to say anything. All she wanted to do was escape, but her feet felt like they were encased in cement. When his hands settled on her hips, her eyes went wide with fear. If only she could bolt for the nearest exit or...

Wake up. Wake up.

It was worth a try. She was sure he could hear her heart hammering inside of her ribcage. The last time he'd touched her in a dream he'd induced excruciating pain. Her nerves were on edge. Did he mean to try and force information from her again? Was this a glimpse into the future hell that awaited her?

He ran his nose up the side of her throat and inhaled deeply, taking in her scent. "I'm hungry." His tone was a blend of sexual arousal and ravenous hunger.

The minute she looked into his eyes his appearance changed to that of his true face: a demonic, feral looking animal. His hands gripped her and kept her from escape and then he plunged his fangs into her neck. She opened her mouth to scream...

"Willow... Willow. Wake up. You're dreaming."

She took a stuttering breath and looked up at Phaedra, who had shaken her awake. Tears glistened in her eyes. Panic still squeezed her like a vise.

"Are you all right?" Phaedra searched her face.

Her hands clutched the armrests in a death grip. It would take a minute before her nerves settled, but she said what came natural. "I'm okay." A weak smile slid into place and she looked away. Phaedra didn't linger, she went back to her seat and left her alone. Willow leaned her head against the back of the seat and felt overwhelming gratitude towards her for not hovering and being over protective.

Once her breathing calmed and her heart returned to a regular rhythm she allowed herself to think about the nightmare. Every time she was in his presence she felt paralyzed. It worried her that when she eventually met the flesh and blood man that the same thing would happen. All of her training would go out the window. She had to learn how to overcome this crippling fright that overtook her when she encountered him in her dreams. If she couldn't do it there, she wouldn't be able to do it for real.

The intermittent clickety clack of the train soothed her after the disturbing dream.

Forty-eight hours ago, they were in Massachusetts and now they were riding Greek Railways from Athens to Delphi. From the moment she told everyone about her mother's letters, they hadn't stopped moving. Planning and preparations were swift. They found a place to leave the Protectors 2.0 RV. Morgana used magic to create passports with fake identities. Tickets were paid for in cash at the airport to avoid a paper trail. Before she knew it they were on a plane. No one questioned her on the legitimacy or validity of the letters. Once she said this was where they needed to be, they'd made it happen.

Eli made a call to his father and The Council reached out to a Greek coven, they would be meeting in Delphi. She was intrigued by The Council's international reach. It stood to reason that if they had supernaturals in America there would be supernaturals all over the world, but she still found it surreal.

In the seat next to her, Eli slept. His hair was mussed and his face was more relaxed than it usually was. Ever since her brush with death he'd taken to wearing casual attire. If she had to confess, as sexy as she'd found the professor look he used to sport, she found him even sexier in the rugged jeans and t-shirt look. She wanted to lean over and kiss him, but she didn't want to wake him. Plus, she was afraid of starting something they couldn't finish. The bathrooms on the train weren't exactly some place she wanted to have a romantic tryst or a quick romp.

If any of the others found the new status of their relationship strange, they didn't say anything. Every now and again, she caught a look being passed between Eli and Phaedra. She was unsure if it had anything to do with the two of them. Sometimes she wanted to pinch herself. She still couldn't believe he loved her. After a quick glance at his sleeping face she returned to her perusal of the countryside.

Ever since she'd read that first letter and learned about The Book of Prophecy, she hadn't been able to stop thinking about it. What did it contain? Where were they going to find it? Her mother's mention of a key still had her puzzled. She twirled the snake pendant on her necklace between her fingers as she pondered over everything.

The few letters she read so far were entrenched in her mind. She'd read them so many times she had them memorized. It was difficult not to rush through them and read them all in one sitting, but she'd disciplined herself to savor each one. Getting the opportunity to communicate with her mother one last time was a gift she didn't want to squander.

Retracing her mother's journey and possibly following the same path she had made her feel even closer to her than she had in a long time.

She pulled one of her mother's previously read letters from her bag. When she took in the dwindling amount she had left to read it made her stomach ache. The letter was heavy in her hands. She looked up. Outside the window, Mount Parnassus loomed in the distance, like a sleeping behemoth. Her eyes returned to the letter. The jagged, broken envelope flap reminded her how many times she'd read and re-read the letter. She took it out and read it for the tenth time.

MAY 17, 2002

Willow, I wish you could see the magnificence that is Greece. It's majestic. If wishes came true my wish would be to be there when you see this place for the first time...

A lump formed in her throat at her mother's wish that would never come true.

Eli stirred next to her. Slowly, he blinked his eyes open and sat up. He rubbed the sleep from his eyes. "Hey." The smile that he gifted her with made her heart somersault in her chest. He leaned over and placed a kiss on her bare shoulder. She found that once he proclaimed his love for her he never seemed to stop touching her. It was a huge contrast to how he used to treat her when duty was the most important thing to him. "Are we close?" He ran a hand through his dark hair.

She looked at her watch. "I think just fifteen to twenty minutes or so."

After stretching his arms over his head, he settled into his seat. "I'm wondering who will be in the welcoming committee. We weren't told who to expect." His gaze dropped to the open letter in her lap.

Embarrassment assailed her. Hastily, she refolded the letter and returned it to the envelope. She wasn't sure why she felt silly for being caught rereading her mother's letters. Eli never judged her or made her feel weird about it.

"Why do you do that?"

"What?" She tried to feign ignorance as she stuffed the envelope into her bag.

"You know what... It's perfectly natural for you to want to read them over and over, but you act like you have to sneak them."

Her eyes looked at the empty chair across the aisle, then wandered to the dusty floor of the railway car, trying to evade his question. He sighed and put his arm around her.

It was nice that he reassured her, but things were so new between them, she wasn't sure which of her quirks would turn him off. Better to tread carefully.

"Looks like we're here." Mathilda announced.

They all peered out the window, hoping to catch a glimpse of whoever was waiting on them. The expectation that they would be wearing black robes and witch hats crossed her mind. She still couldn't help equating the cliché uniform to witches.

No one stood out from the crowd so they gathered their things and exited the train. When they stepped onto the train platform, the strong scent of pine floated by on the breeze. She closed her eyes and inhaled deeply, taking in the smell of diesel fuel that now co-mingled with pine. Her nose wrinkled in distaste.

"Are you the Oracle?" An excited, nervous voice that bordered on the hysteria of fangirling caused her to open her eyes. A voluptuous brunette was invading her personal space, staring at her with wide, curious eyes.

Eli and Max flanked her on either side. Max emitted a low growl that would be imperceptible to most. They must have perceived the woman as a threat.

"Who wants to know?" After the last ambush, she was a bit skittish around strangers. The now healed scar twinged with pain at the thought. It had to be psychological since she hadn't experienced any pain since they healed her.

"It's her. It's her." The woman hopped up and down with unconcealed enthusiasm.

Willow tried to take a step back, but was wrapped up in a hug that threatened to choke the life out of her.

"Let the poor woman go, Nyssa, she needs to breathe." The Greek accented voice was only half joking. Once Nyssa released her she was able to tilt her head back to look at the giant of a man that had spoken. "Please forgive her. No one here has seen an Oracle for over a thousand years. In ancient times, Delphi was considered the center of the world. This city had tremendous religious and political influence because kings, generals, common people, traveled from all over the world to seek the Oracle's wisdom on matters that ranged from the mundane to whether to wage war on another nation. She transcended cultural boundaries." His face beamed with awe. "So, here in Greece, you can imagine how excited we are at the prospect of meeting you."

Willow could only gawk at him. Not only because of how prolific the Oracle was, but because the man looked like a human bear. At a minimum, he was 6'7" and had the build of a defensive lineman. His arms, legs and any other place where his skin was visible were covered in coarse black hairs. His face appeared under siege from the bushy beard and caterpillar brows. The only place that was devoid of hair was his bald head.

Once she got over the shock of his size, she realized that their group consisted of more than this man and the woman he'd called Nyssa. Another man and woman stood off to the side. Before she could respond or the man could continue, Eli intervened.

"I thought our arrival was going to be kept secret." He didn't try to mask the agitation in his voice.

"Oopsie." The man shrugged, but didn't seem apologetic. "It is hard to keep secrets in this small town. Everyone has been very excited as you can see." He nodded in Nyssa's direction to prove his point. Their heads swiveled to gaze at the woman who was so rabid with glee she practically foamed at the mouth.

"You know how the supernatural community can be."
He lightly punched Eli on the arm in camaraderie.

She didn't realize she'd been holding her breath, until
she saw Eli's tense stance relax. "I'm Eli, the head of the
Protectors... and you are?" He extended his hand towards
the human bear.

The giant grinned broadly at them and clasped Eli's
hand in a friendly gesture. "My name is Arsenio. I'm part of
the Castellanos coven."

Max must have been in her head, because instantly
after hearing the man's name he blurted out what she was
thinking. "Arsenio? As in the 90s late night talk show
host?"

Please do not offend this man.

If she had better command of her telepathic ability like
Eli she would tell Max to keep whatever jokes he was about
to make to himself. Although Phaedra was on the other
side of Max, it was clear she tried to shush him by elbowing
him because he winced in discomfort and clutched his
stomach. The deterrent seemed to work because Max
didn't offer up any more jokes.

Arsenio had a great sense of humor because he let out a
hearty laugh. "I get that all the time from Americans.
Arsenio is a Greek name. It has been used in my family for
generations. I was named after one of my uncles,
Arsenios." He let go of Eli's hand and took a step back.
"Come. Let me introduce the others."

CHAPTER 2

Eli

"**YOU ALREADY KNOW** Nyssa." The tall, curvy woman smiled and gave a little wave, but her eyes never left Willow. Still he wondered if he needed to be concerned.

"This is Damaris." Arsenio beckoned the petite, black haired beauty forward. Where Nyssa seemed to display every emotion like a human video billboard, Damaris was reserved. He didn't like that he couldn't read her.

"Geia sas." She smiled at all of them, but returned her gaze to Willow.

"Damaris and Nyssa are maenads."

"What?" Willow asked and her eyes blinked in rapid succession while she tried to make sense of what Arsenio had revealed about his companions.

"Maenads are priestesses of Dionysus." Mathilda volunteered, clearly as awestruck as Willow was herself.

"Okay." It was evident she was still unsure what to make of the two women. He had to fight the urge to smile.

"YOU WANT TO ASK MORE QUESTIONS SO BADLY. I KNOW YOU DO." He joked with her telepathically.

"OF COURSE I DO. WHAT THE HELL IS A MAENAD? MATHILDA ACTS LIKE THAT EXPLANATION SUMMED UP EVERYTHING I NEEDED TO KNOW. I'M STILL CLUELESS."

His eyes went wide with amusement and he coughed to cover the laugh that slipped out. "Road dust... Just have a touch of it scratching my throat." He explained while he coughed and cleared his throat when everyone looked at him. Out of the corner of his eye, he caught Willow sporting a smirk at his lame excuse.

"This fellow is Ulrik. He's a vampire and has been a guest of the supernatural community here in Delphi for over a year now." Arsenio continued with his introductions.

The man that stepped forward, looked like he was a Viking in another life. In the sea of dark hair and swarthy skin, he stuck out for his fair skin and honey blonde hair. He formally bowed and then proceeded to kiss the hand of each of the female Protectors. Maybe Ulrik was an Old World vampire because he was very formal. All of the women, with the exception of Phaedra, swooned at the gesture, including Willow he noticed. "Hej. It is a pleasure to meet you all." The Danish accent had them all dreamy eyed.

Some of the women may have been taken in by his charms, but he and Phaedra shared a look at hearing he was a vampire. He was definitely interested to know how a lone vampire ended up in Greece. Arsenio mentioned he was a guest here. He hoped Ulrik would have no problem sharing his story later when he asked him. Until then, Eli planned to be on high alert. For all they knew, he could be a mole planted by Killian. He didn't want to be paranoid, but it was Willow's life that was at stake. He'd rather be safe than sorry.

Eli let everyone introduce themselves. He was no one's mouthpiece. Plus, he didn't know what the women were liable to do to him if he tried.

Once all the pleasantries were out of the way, Arsenio barked some orders in Greek, "Párte tis tsántes tous tóra." A few men materialized from nowhere and grabbed their luggage.

The men scuttled away and they followed.

Willow leaned over and whispered in his ear, "Okay, now that no one can overhear me asking you, tell me what exactly are maenads?"

He grinned. "Mathilda was correct, they're priestesses of Dionysus who was the Greek god of wine..."

She interrupted him. "I thought that was Bacchus?"

"That's his name in Roman mythology. Anyways, over the years it got boiled down to the maenads goal being to get you to drink and reach a greater state of ecstasy."

When he looked at her to see if she was satisfied with his answer she raised an eyebrow. "I don't see what all the fuss is about."

"There was stuff about ripping bull's apart and drinking blood so you could be possessed by Dionysus."

She wrinkled her nose and looked slightly alarmed. Maybe his explanation was deeper than it needed to be.

"Think about it this way, if a party was a dud, bring in some maenads, it won't be a dud for much longer. They're kind of like people that amp up the fun level on a party."

"So they get people turnt up?"

Her succinct explanation made him chuckle. "That's a great way to put it. Now multiple what your idea of that is by like 10,000."

She looked over her shoulder at Nyssa and Damaris. "So this banquet is gonna be lit tonight because of those two?" She turned back to him. "I don't see it." She snorted in disbelief.

Parked at the curb were five identical, gray Peugeot 308 hatchbacks. The drivers loaded all of the baggage into one of the cars.

"Get in. Get in. Let us be off." Arsenio urged everyone to get into the vehicles.

He and Willow climbed into the backseat of Arsenio's car. Phaedra and Max ended up in the car with Nyssa, which made him want to laugh, thinking about how

Phaedra would respond to the bubbly maenad. Morgana, Mathilda and Ulrik grabbed the next car and Zoriana and Damaris rode in the last car.

As they pulled away from the station, Arsenio talked from the passenger seat. Given his large frame, it was impossible for him to turn around and address them so he spoke loudly. "You couldn't have chosen a better time to come to Delphi. The Pythian Games are starting soon and everyone's excited to have the Oracle preside over the games. It's why the maenads accompanied me to pick you up. They wish to throw a banquet tonight in your honor."

Eli glanced over at Willow to gauge her reaction to all of this. Her mouth was hanging open like she was waiting to catch some flies.

"What?" She shook herself. "What?"

"Maybe you won't get that Grammy, but it looks like you'll get to live like a rock star while we're here." He smiled at her.

It was clear she was trying to contain the excitement bubbling up inside of her. She bit her lip and tried to fight back the huge grin that wouldn't go away. She leaned into him and whispered. "Do you think they'll let me perform?"

"You're the Oracle. I don't think they'd deny you anything. You saw the way that chick Nyssa was about to faint after catching a glimpse of you." He chuckled and brushed a few curls out of her face. When he peered at her, it warmed his heart to see worry lines weren't etched into her forehead and her face was devoid of concern and battle fatigue. It made him happy that she might get to have a bit of fun. Yeah they were here for a purpose, but she deserved a night off from everything. Even though they were celebrating the Oracle, she could pretend they were honoring her as a singer instead. He kissed her forehead. Something flipped in his stomach when he heard her blissful sigh and she snuggled into his side; then she was off with a million questions for Arsenio.

"What are the Pythian Games?"

"You have not educated her thoroughly on her history, Eli."

"Sorry, it's been hard finding time to go over ancient Greek history while eluding bloodthirsty vampires." His voice dripped with sarcasm, which seemed to be lost on Arsenio because he only tsked and proceeded to give her a detailed account of what exactly the Pythian Games were.

"The Pythian Games are similar to the Olympics, but were held in honor of Apollo. Delphi hosted these athletic events: chariot races, wrestling, boxing, horse races and such, every two years after the Olympics. Initially, it started out with competitions in art: singing, dancing, poetry, before the athletic events were added..." the man continued on. After Arsenio's speech on the platform about how important the Oracle was, you'd think he would have remembered the guy was a bit of a history buff.

Every now and then, Willow interrupted him, but he didn't seem to mind the endless questions that she threw at him. Eli had to admit, he was a little rusty on his Greek history so he rather enjoyed Arsenio's recap. The man was a master storyteller. He half wished they were sitting around a campfire with some S'mores.

After a while, his attention was drawn elsewhere. He listened to the two of them prattle on while he enjoyed gazing out the window at the countryside. Among the abundance of pine trees he saw fig and olive trees also dotted the valley. Wherever they were headed must have been on the outskirts of town, because they passed through without stopping. It made sense that the supernaturals would want to avoid attention.

Thirty minutes later they pulled up to a compound with a security gate. Arsenio waved his hand and repeated some Latin phrase he couldn't hear and the gate slid open. Their caravan rolled through the gate and drove down a driveway that ran for about half a mile before they arrived at a sprawling estate nestled among pine trees. The white stucco villa was modern in its design. Once the cars parked along the circular driveway, everyone got out.

"Sweet." Max was clearly impressed with their Greek accommodations.

Standing in front of the house were two tall men with the musculature of Hercules. They were identical. The only way to tell they'd seen at least forty plus birthdays was the gray at their temples and the crow's feet that crinkled at the corners of their eyes. Their skin was deeply tan. It was hard to tell if it was natural or if the men enjoyed lying about in the sun or a tanning bed.

"Who are they?" Willow asked Arsenio as they climbed from the car.

Eli's attention was drawn to them as well. There was something about the insolence and smugness that marred the one man's face that reminded him of his father. He found himself taking an instant dislike to that one. Of course he chided himself for being childish instead of waiting to reserve judgment. Although, he often found his first instincts were usually right. The other one had a strange look on his face as he stared into the car. Almost like he was looking at a ghost.

"That's Lysander and Hadrian. They are twin brother and the heads of our coven." Before Arsenio could walk them over and introduce them, Lysander said something to Hadrian and walked away, disappearing around the side of the house. Hadrian's eyes didn't leave Willow the whole time they approached him. It made Eli uneasy. Not that he deemed Hadrian or Lysander a threat... yet. It's just the look in Hadrian's eyes didn't quite match the smile on his face. He wasn't sure what to make of it. Right now he would try and relax, for her.

Tonight they would have a good time and then they needed to get down to the business of finding that book. Hyacinth's letter said that Killian already knew of the book, which meant that he could already have people on the ground here scavenging for it. His mind went to Ulrik again. He planned to have a conversation with him tonight. Between Ulrik and Damaris, he planned to make sure that neither posed a threat to Willow or their mission to find the book. It was possible he might need to add Hadrian or Lysander to that list. If so, it didn't matter if there were peace treaties in place, he would raise hell if any harm came to a hair on her head. Consequences be damned.

CHAPTER 3

Willow

THE WAY HIS eyes never left her made her feel a bit uncomfortable, but not in a sleazy sort of way. It was like they were probing, trying to uncover something hidden. When they finally stood in front of him, he continued to peer at her without blinking. He hadn't acknowledged Eli's presence yet.

"Hadrian, this is..."

"Eli. Pleased to meet you." Without waiting for Arsenio to make the introductions, Eli cut him off by sticking his hand in Hadrian's face. The man was forced to look at him.

She exhaled a breath she didn't realize she'd been holding while under his scrutiny.

"It was very kind of you to offer us hospitality while we're here in Greece."

She cut her eye at Eli and wondered what he was up to. He didn't normally make a bunch of small talk and offer pleasantries. If she had to hazard a guess she wondered if he'd been jealous over how Hadrian had been watching her. It's not like anyone could have missed that his eyes were glued to her. She couldn't help smirking at the thought of a jealous Eli. Later, she would tease him unmercifully about it.

Everyone else walked up behind them and Eli told them to introduce themselves. He put his arm around her and pulled her close. The only thing that saved him from being slapped or told off after displaying his need to claim her and mark her as his territory like a piece of cattle was when he looked at her with such a humbling smile. Even though he spoke no words, his expression seemed to tell her that he knew she was the catch and he was lucky to have her. It was hard not to get lost in his dreamy blue eyes. She was glad she wouldn't have to stuff his toxic masculinity down his throat later.

Once everyone finished telling Hadrian who they were, he turned his attention back to her, like she was the only guest.

"Welcome to the Castellanos Villa. I hope you will be very comfortable here. Rooms have been made up. Arsenio will see you settled." He took his eyes off of her to nod in the giant's direction like they didn't know who Arsenio was. Then Hadrian looked around at the group. "I do hope everything is to your liking. We've hired extra staff to help you get ready for tonight's festivities." His gaze returned to her. "In your room, you'll find a gift. A dress for tonight."

For a minute, his look was so intimate, she was afraid he would lift her hand and kiss it and earn a karate chop to the throat from Eli.

"Thank you." She squeaked out.

"For all of you, we have provided clothing for tonight. We want you to feel most welcome." His attention returned to the group once more, then he stepped aside so Arsenio could walk them into the house. She didn't need to turn around to know his eyes watched her. Reflexively, she cuddled closer to Eli.

Arsenio grabbed a key from his pocket and stepped forward. Once again she noticed the door only had a knocker. Unlike the one on the Walker house, this one was made from gold and in the shape of the Hecate symbol, the goddess of witchcraft. She only knew what that looked like because of reading over Mathilda's shoulder occasionally on the plane. The minute the door sensed his key a keyhole appeared exactly as it had at the Walker house. He inserted the key and the door opened.

Inside the open floor plan villa, the décor was a multitude of white with accents of cool earth tones and touches of turquoise. In the living room area the French doors that led to a patio and terrace were thrown wide and a gentle breeze blew. He guided them back outdoors where the terrace turned into an enormous courtyard that seemed to connect some of the other buildings. In the center was a swimming pool. Lounge chairs for sunbathing and umbrellas dotted the area. It felt like a luxury hotel and not a witches' house. It was a huge contrast to the centuries old clapboard house the Walker coven occupied in Salem.

"Phaedra and Max, I do believe you'll be most comfortable in the outdoor bungalow." He motioned towards the guesthouse.

No one needed to tell those two twice. Max bounded after Phaedra towards the place where they would be afforded some privacy.

Mathilda stepped forward. "Will I have my own room?"

The teenager could have slapped her mother and it wouldn't have delivered quite the sting her comment had. Arsenio seemed to falter for a moment. A first, since she'd met him. "I'd assumed..." He looked back and forth between mother and daughter, at a loss for words. Eli was angry and about to speak up when Morgana stepped forward.

"Totally fine. Mathilda and I can share. It will be like one big non-stop slumber party." Morgana squeezed Zoriana's shoulder before walking up and standing next to Mathilda. "Just lead the way."

Arsenio pointed out a bedroom in another direction that was just off the courtyard.

She couldn't bring herself to look at Zoriana's face as she watched her daughter walk away without a backwards glance.

That was brutal.

Thankfully, they didn't have to endure the awkwardness too long. "Your rooms are just inside, if you would follow me." They followed him back into the house where he delivered Zoriana to her room first before leading them to a suite. With great flare, like he was opening the door to a palace, Arsenio threw open the double doors that led to their room. The bedroom was vast. Her whole apartment back in Nashville could have fit inside the room. She almost missed the three steps that led down into the room when her eyes landed on four nearly nude men. They looked like they had tanned in the sun and then been oiled down. Muscles bulged here and there, chiseled six-pack abs taunted her and the teeny tiny shorts they sported left nothing to the imagination. They were all well endowed.

"I apologize. When we set things up we had no idea the two of you were... together. They were here to bathe you and take care of your needs for tonight's party."

It wasn't everyday someone offered her semi-nude male servants to do her bidding. If she wasn't already very satisfied and happy with Eli she would have jumped at the opportunity to be the mistress of a harem for the night.

"I'm more than capable of taking care of her needs." When she looked at Eli his jaw was clenched and his brows were creased together in an angry scowl.

"I'll just see them out. I'm sure some of the other ladies could use some pampering after your trip."

Once Arsenio left with the buff male staff in tow, she burst out laughing and fell on the bed.

"What's so funny?"

"You are babe. You know I don't want any of them right? I mean they're cute in all, but you're all the eye candy I need." She got up from the bed and took his hands in hers.

"Oh really? Because I could have picked your chin up off the floor and tucked your tongue back in your mouth you were drooling so hard. Maybe I should go ask Arsenio if there were some naked women waiting in the room he had for me." He teased her and acted like he was going to go after them.

"Stop." She giggled and wrapped her arms around his waist. "It's true. You are the only thing I need."

He pulled her closer, while he glanced over her shoulder. "I think I see a rather large bathing pool in the bathroom, maybe we should test it out before tonight?"

It sounded like a good time, but she couldn't help stifling a yawn. 'Yes, let's do that."

He leaned down to kiss her, but she yawned even bigger before his lips could land on hers.

"Maybe, you should get some rest. We traveled for a long time. You must be exhausted."

"I'm sorry. I really want to." Her hand covered her mouth as she fought off yet another yawn.

He smiled. "We can try it out tonight." He dropped a kiss on her forehead. "Lay down and get some rest."

She didn't argue with him and allowed him to lead her to the bed. Many thoughts flitted through her mind in her drowsy state.

The entire trip felt like a dream. It wasn't just the dinner they were throwing in her honor, but there was this tug in her spirit from the moment they landed in Athens that became even more amplified the closer they got to Delphi. It ran bone deep... no deeper than that, like it was tethered to the cells that made up her body, her very DNA. There was no other way to express it, other than to say the feeling was like she had finally arrived home. She hadn't felt that way since her mother passed.

She didn't remember hearing him tell her, 'Sweet dreams,' before she succumbed to a deep sleep.

CHAPTER 4

Eli

SHE SHOOED HIM out of the suite when three women showed up after her nap to help her get ready. Arsenio had shown him to the room that was meant to be his and he'd showered and changed into the garments Hadrian provided. The beige linen pants and long sleeved, white tunic style shirt weren't items he would have chosen for himself, but the lightweight fabrics did help him stay cool in the balmy weather.

He paced the floor as he waited for her. Arsenio had already whisked the rest of the group away to the location where the banquet was to be held. The supernaturals here had really rolled out the red carpet for her. With all this luxury and being pampered and waited on hand and foot it was so easy to want to treat this like some vacation. He wanted her to have her fun, but he didn't want them to lose sight of why they were here. They had to find that book before Killian did. After tonight he needed to make sure they got back on track.

Just as he was about to pace the length of the living room once more, she entered, and what an entrance it was. He halted mid-step. His eyes took in the goddess they'd transformed her into. She'd always been beautiful to him, but tonight she looked like she belonged in a classic film about ancient Greece.

The white, one shoulder, female toga she wore was trimmed in gold. It hugged and accentuated her curves to perfection and was cinched with a skinny, gold belt. The skirt of the toga fell to her ankles, but there were slits up the sides, so when she moved you were treated to a display of her long gorgeous legs. Her feet were clad in gladiator style sandals with thin golden straps that wound themselves around her legs up to her calf muscle. The women had styled her curls in a slightly messy updo and then crowned it with a laurel wreath. Her face appeared to be dusted in gold leaf. At different moments the light reflected her face glittering, depending on the way she turned.

"Do you like it?" She looked down at herself and smoothed out an invisible wrinkle and fussed over her hair.

"You look... you look... words can't describe how you look." He said with awe staining his words. Her eyes finally met his and he placed his hand over his heart.

When she leaned in and kissed him, his hands slid up and held her face in his palms as he gave her a lingering, unhurried kiss. He wished they didn't have to go. As beautiful as she looked, suddenly all he wanted to do was take her to bed and stay there for hours. He broke the kiss and leaned his forehead against hers. He panted slightly. "We should go."

In the car, they sat close to each other and talked and laughed. He could feel the excitement and curiosity that coursed through her as they sat shoulder-to-shoulder and thigh-to-thigh. Her excitement made him just a bit giddy.

"The ladies who helped me get ready tonight said this banquet is called a bachnal or something like that." The perplexed look on her face was adorable.

"It's Bacchanalia... The Greco-Roman god of wine I mentioned earlier, it was in honor of him. It's come to have a lot of interpretations over the years," He wasn't sure he wanted to tell her it was believed to have possibly been some secret cult initiation event that included drunken orgies. "Just think of it as one hell of a party."

When the car stopped, they got out and saw large white tents in the middle of a valley surrounded by mountains. Walking through the tent, which posed as an entrance to the festivities, they could hear laughter, talking and live music. Once they walked through they could see everything was set up outdoors, underneath the stars. Long, low tables were set up with thick cushions being used for seating.

At the head table, he could see Phaedra and Max on one side and Morgana, Zoriana and Mathilda on one side, with Morgana in the middle of course. Hadrian, Lysander, Arsenio and Ulrik also sat at the table. He noticed the vacant seats that were meant for them were between Hadrian and Ulrik.

This is definitely going to be an interesting evening.

At least he was going to get the opportunity to ask about Ulrik's past.

As they seated themselves, Max raised his glass towards them. "All I can say is if being part of your entourage gets us this kind of VIP treatment; count me in."

Morgana and Mathilda giggled at him. Phaedra rolled her eyes while she tried to suppress a smirk.

Hadrian made sure that Willow was seated next to him. "You look lovely."

"Thank you and thank you for the beautiful outfit." Even though she addressed Hadrian, she leaned into him. The man looked at her like a lion looking at a snack before he stood and clapped his hands together. Everyone fell silent.

"Invited guests, we're gathered here tonight in honor of our Mistress of Ceremonies, who will preside over the Pythian Games. The one true Oracle, Ms. Willow Stevens." The audience applauded and whistled.

Eli looked out at the crowd and wondered who all was in attendance from the supernatural community. He was sure most if not all of these people were in some way affiliated with the supernatural world or Hadrian would have never announced her as the Oracle.

"We are honored to have her with us tonight." Hadrian extended his hand to her.

Eli could see Willow was nervous when she looked to him instead of taking Hadrian's hand and standing. It was unlike her. He gave her a quick kiss and reassured her. "You're going to do great."

She turned back to Hadrian and took his offered hand. He pulled her to her feet and the applause grew thunderous.

"I've been told she would like to grace us with a song." He addressed the crowd once more, while still gripping her hand in his. Before the applause completely died away, he kissed her on the cheek and released her. After he reclaimed his seat, she was left standing in the spotlight alone.

"Oh wow... I didn't realize I would be singing right away." She looked around. "Where's a microphone?" She directed the question at Hadrian.

"You don't need one." He waved his hand over her. "Amplifico. Now your voice is amplified enough for everyone to hear you. Sing."

Willow looked at him once more and he smiled and blew her a kiss. She turned back to the crowd and cleared her throat before launching into a kickass rendition of 'I Want You To Want Me' that got everyone on their feet. Hadrian was right, there was no need for a microphone, because the spell he cast, amplified her voice and allowed her voice to carry out across the hordes of people that had come for tonight's festivities. People danced and sang along as her voice dazzled and mesmerized them. When she finished the applause was deafening.

The smile she wore was huge. "That was crazy." She half whispered to him. "They loved it." Clearly, all the attention she was receiving was taking some time to sink in.

"They love you." He told her. He couldn't take his eyes off of her. She was radiant.

"You have the voice of a siren. You could lure a man to his death, my dear." Hadrian kissed the back of her hand and then he was on his feet again. "Thank you, Willow. Let the Bacchanalia begin." Hadrian's announcement was met with more raucous cheers and whistles.

Seconds later, Nyssa, Damaris and what he was guessing were more maenads took the floor. All of the women were very attractive. They wore cropped tops that bared their midriff, flowing skirts and veils. Once they were all assembled, a live band began to play music and the women danced.

The women swiveled their hips in a suggestive manner to the beat of the music. The dance they performed hyped the crowd into a frenzy. Soon people were up and moving. The dancers moved among the crowd, encouraging people still in their seats to get up. No prodding was needed for Hadrian, Lysander or Arsenio to join in the fun. They quickly left the table. He noticed Damaris take Hadrian's hand, before they were swallowed up by the crowd.

Are they a couple?

He had no time to ponder the thought, because it wasn't long before someone approached their table and enticed Willow to join the revelry. "They want me to join them."

"Go. Go have fun. I'll be waiting right here when you come back." He looked over and noticed that Ulrik wasn't planning to join in the merrymaking. "I'm going to have a little chat with Ulrik." He patted her thigh.

She grinned at him before she stood and ran off with a bunch of party-goers.

"I think I'm going to call it a night." Zoriana gathered her things.

"Are you sure?" It was hard not to be concerned for her well-being.

"Yeah, I'm fine. Not my scene. Maybe if Alistair were here..." She looked in the direction Mathilda and Morgana headed to join other revelers. "I think I'm going to go back

MONI BOYCE

to the villa and have a long soak in the huge bathtub." She gave him a wan smile. If things were different between her and Mathilda, he knew she would have stayed.

"Okay." He watched her walk away.

Max stood and tugged on Phaedra's arm. She looked towards him. "When in Rome..." A small grin lifted the corner of her mouth before she left her seat and followed Max into the throng.

"Tell me about yourself." His attention returned to the silent vampire.

"You've been trying to figure me out since you met me. Trying to see if you need to watch me. Am I a traitor and spy or friend?" Ulrik gave him a look of amusement.

"Well you've made this a lot easier." Eli folded his arms across his chest. "So, which is it?"

Ulrik laughed briefly before he grew serious. "I've been a vampire for a long time. Killian wasn't always king. You're too young to know of a time when vampires did work and live in harmony with other supernaturals." He adjusted himself on his cushion so he was facing Eli. "When Killian seized control, it was like watching Hitler rise to power all over again. Only instead of white supremacy it was vampire supremacy." The look on the Dane's face was one of distaste and disgust. "His regime is very loyal to him."

34

Despite the laughter and pulsing music that surrounded them, Eli was focused on the story Ulrik weaved.

"When relationships and communications between anyone that wasn't a vampire became forbidden, I knew I wouldn't last much longer... you see, my brother is a werewolf."

It had been a while since Eli had been surprised, but he arched his eyebrows in surprise over Ulrik's admission.

"Not many others knew, but I knew it was only a matter of time before more found out and they targeted me. I was never a big supporter of Killian, but being an older vampire gave me some clout. With that knowledge, not even my seniority would save me. Someone would trade that information to gain favor. They would force my loyalty and allegiance. It would come down to execution or excommunication. It was an easy decision to make. So here I am." He drained his wine glass.

"When I arrived here, many wondered like you, whether I could be trusted. It took a while for me to be fully accepted here, but I have been."

The two of them eyed each other.

"Have I passed your test? Can I be trusted?" He gifted Eli with a wry grin.

Eli pursed his lips and looked over the man as he thought. "For now."

Ulrik threw his head back and laughed. "Then let's toast to our new friendship. More wine." He called out to a passing server, who left a wine bottle. Ulrik poured them each a full glass. They toasted and the blonde vampire tipped his back and drank down the contents.

Eli took a healthy swallow and then sat the glass down. He was a little surprised when Ulrik started speaking again.

"Fanden..." He said the Danish swear word in a low voice to himself before he addressed Eli again. "You know, I thought I'd escaped all the prejudices and superiority bullshit until a few months ago. I overheard some idiots talking about getting rid of hybrid supernaturals. As the saying goes, 'Everywhere you go, there you are.' Right? No escaping it. Different location, but the same old shit. I've been hearing talk of them calling themselves Supernaturals Against Hybrids or some such nonsense. I want to find those bastards and crack their skulls." Clearly, the wine was loosening his tongue.

Eli decided to take advantage and ask more questions. In case, sobriety made him clam up later. Despite the party that raged around him, he was all business. "Can you tell me about a female vampire that is of Middle Eastern descent, looks like she could be a model? I believe she's pretty close to Killian."

Ulrik snorted. "That would be Katana." The grimace that sat upon his face told Eli, Ulrik had had the pleasure of her acquaintance. "You've had a run in with her?"

Eli nodded.

"Møgkælling. She's a nasty piece of work." His expression looked as though he was remembering something unpleasant. "The story goes that sometime during the seventeenth or eighteenth century, Killian wasn't king yet, but he was still a powerful vampire. A maharaja visited him and gifted him with Katana. She was part of his harem, a concubine it was said. I'm not sure." He refilled his wine glass. "She was caught being unfaithful. That was the story the maharaja gave Killian. The truth was she had been spirited away on her wedding day before the ceremony because the maharaja wanted her. After being forced into his harem, she tried to escape months later to run away with the man that should have been her husband. They were caught. He was killed and she was demoted and forced to be the plaything for the maharaja's men."

Ulrik sipped his wine and glanced at the debauchery happening around them. He turned his gaze back to Eli. "A short while after the maharaja's visit Killian set her free. She'd come to learn what he was and begged him to make her a vampire too so she could vanquish her enemy. She vowed if he helped her she would pledge her life to him. He turned her. They sailed to India and dined on the maharaja and his entire household over the course of seven days. She's been by his side, doing his bidding ever since."

After he finished, Eli drank down the rest of his wine. Hearing Katana's origin gave him perspective on who she was. He understood now who he was dealing with when it came to her. His eyes scanned the crowd. Most seemed to have lost their inhibitions as the night wore on. Many were intoxicated, whether it was on the alcohol that flowed, drugs or just the vibe the maenads gave off, he wasn't sure. Drunken dancers still gyrated and moved to the music. Clothes had come off, leaving some in a semi-nude state. Some were having sex on tables, on the ground, in couples, threesomes, orgies. He grew concerned for Willow. Mathilda was with Morgana, so he wasn't alarmed, knowing that Morgana would keep her safe. He was about to go in search of Willow when she stumbled over.

"Dance with me." Willow took his hands and attempted to pull him up from the cushion. There was a sultry, seductive quality to her voice that quickly had him assessing her. The maenads seemed to be having an effect on her too. He hoped it was them and not something someone might have slipped her. The maenads effect would wear off after a few hours when they were out of their proximity. He resisted.

"Come on. Dance with me. Loosen up a little bit." She released his hand and stepped back. Her body swayed to some rhythm only she could hear. A guy wandered up and pulled her back against his body. They needed to get out of here before he beat someone within an inch of their life.

He turned to Ulrik. "Could you see that Morgana and Mathilda get back to the villa safely? I know Max and Phaedra can take care of themselves."

"Sure. Anything for you, my friend." Ulrik raised his glass to him.

Eli came over and started dancing with her. He gave the other guy a death glare that sent him scurrying away. Willow put her arms around his neck and he pulled her close. She ground her hips into him and instantly he was hard. Maybe it was the crowd. It was more than likely the mood the maenads created, but he was intoxicated with lust. He was inches away from ripping Willow's clothes off her body and fucking her right here on the ground. A small semblance of control shined through despite his swelling manhood. "Why don't we go back to the villa and we can finish what I tried to start earlier?" He whispered in her ear as he ran his fingers up and down her back. She pulled him down for a kiss and he knew it was time to leave.

CHAPTER 5

Willow

THEY FELL INTO the room groping and kissing. She unfastened her toga as they stumbled down the steps towards the bed. The top part of the dress slipped to her waist. Eli sat on the edge of the bed and watched her undress. She went slowly and enjoyed having his eyes on her. When she went to remove the laurel wreath from her hair he spoke. "Don't. Leave it on, the sandals too. It will be like making love to my own goddess."

She smiled at him and walked over and straddled his lap. He leaned back on the bed, bracing his outstretched arms behind him on the bed. For a moment they both just looked at each other. Then a wicked smile took over her face and he grinned back at her. She swiped her tongue across his lips and continued to tease him several times before she finally sunk her teeth into his bottom lip. When the bite elicited a grunt from him, she couldn't wipe the pleased look off of her face. Once she released his lip she sucked it into her mouth to soothe the sting. He wrapped an arm around her and in a swift movement reversed their positions so she now lay beneath him. It was clear he'd had enough of her torment.

His fingers tweaked one of her pebbled nipples while he kissed her roughly. Something in tonight's festivities had brought out the animal in both of them. The only word she could use to describe the mood was primal.

Eli backed away to remove his clothes and put on a condom. He left her spread eagle on the bed. This time there was no sexy striptease. Later she would wonder if he used magic to get out of his clothes he removed them so quickly, then he was on her again. His thick, throbbing member pressed into her belly. It felt like he scalded her with his need to be inside of her. His mouth descended on hers in a feral kiss and she scratched her nails down his back in response.

"Ahhh." His sigh of enjoyment over her clawing his flesh spurred her on. Her teeth sank into his shoulder. The sharp, little bite made him grunt again in pleasure. She smiled against his skin. In a quick maneuver, he flipped her onto her stomach and his body pressed her into the mattress. Her sensitive nipples ached from rubbing against the sheet. His cock rested between the valley of her ass cheeks and he stroked back and forth. Both of them enjoyed the friction and the promise of things yet to come.

She was so wet, she was sure there was a wet spot on the sheets beneath her. A low growl left his throat and then he nipped her neck causing her to cry out.

"I'm gonna take you rough baby. I hope you're ready for me." His voice was husky and gravelly. It was the only warning he gave before he plunged his throbbing member into her balls deep, in one swift motion. He gave a savage roar at being impaled inside her honeyed walls. She clutched the sheets sure she was going to tear a hole in them, as his cock scythed in and out of her. His hands gripped her hips, near to the point of bruising and he pounded into her over and over.

"Fuck!" he bellowed.

It bordered on pleasure and pain, with pleasure winning out with each drugging stroke. "More." She pleaded, hoping his answering response would be to continue to punish her with his dick.

He gave her exactly what she wanted. It felt so good and soon she felt herself hurtling towards her climax. She could tell he was close too. If she could have prolonged it she would have. Before that thought could complete itself, she exploded around his cock. Her walls spasmed and milked his cock, sending him over the edge. A long satisfied groan dropped from his lips as he released into the condom. His forehead rested against her back for a few seconds while he collected himself. Then he pushed from her body to discard the condom.

She panted against the pillow, her ass still up in the air, when she heard the rip of a second condom wrapper. Suddenly, she was hoisted up in his arms. "I'm not done with you, baby." He walked towards the giant bathroom that had a bathing pool in the center. "I've been wanting to take you in this pool since I saw it earlier." He readjusted her so her legs hugged his waist. His hands gripped her ass and he walked down the steps that led into the water. The temperature was just right.

Their mouths fused together in a searing kiss. Soon they were waist deep in the water. He carried her over to the side and pressed her against the wall. They spent the next couple hours christening the bathing pool.

The soggy sandals and laurel wreath were discarded on the floor on the way back to the bed after their wet sexcapades. Damp bed sheets clung to her skin. Her wet curls lay across the pillow. Every part of her was exhausted and sated. It was some of the most mind-blowing sex she'd ever had in her life. Plus, Eli had been an animal. She smiled to herself, reliving the events in the bed and in the bathing pool.

Although, she'd thoroughly enjoyed herself, she felt like she'd had an out of body experience, like she was coming down off some high. Why did she feel like that? She didn't remember taking anything.

Does he feel like that too?

Eli lay on his stomach with his eyes closed. The question she was going to ask flew out of her head when her eyes landed on his naked ass, which was displayed gloriously. Even though they'd just been at it for hours she felt something stir in her nether region. She propped herself up on her side and leaned on her elbow while she admired his body. He must have sensed her watching him. "You like what you see?" He mumbled into the pillow he cradled.

"MmmHmm." She licked her lips.

He opened his eyes and smirked.

"For a white boy, you have a gorgeous ass."

He looked over his shoulder at his naked rear end and then back at her. "I'm glad you like it, baby, but I think you have a better ass." He leaned up and kissed her. She was hoping it was about to turn into round three, but Eli pulled away and turned serious. If he had been affected by anything at the party it had sense worn off.

"Something Ulrik said tonight has me a little on edge, so I need you to do something for me."

"Okay." A little knot of fear curled inside her stomach.

"Don't say anything about being half-fae right now. In my talk with Ulrik, he mentioned some anti-hybrid talk that was going around. I just want to be safe."

She nodded. She could see he was worried. Another time, she might have pushed back, but this wasn't a joke. If he feared for her safety, that someone would harm her if they found out she was part fae, she was going to take it seriously.

He got up from the bed and rummaged in his bag. The smile returned to her face as she was treated to a full view of his sexy body. She sat up trying to see what he was doing.

What is he searching for?

When he came back to the bed, he placed her dagger in her hands. Her mouth fell open in surprise. She thought it was lost forever after that day.

"You found it?" She looked up at him.

He scooted closer to her. "Yeah... shortly before we left the campsite that day. I said I would give it back to you when you recovered. I'd almost forgotten about it. I found it in my bag while you were sleeping this afternoon." His eyes were so earnest. She knew talking about that still made him upset.

"Thank you." She leaned over and kissed him.

"Promise me when you're out and about you'll have it with you."

"I promise." She made sure he heard the sincerity in her response.

"We should probably get some sleep. We have training tomorrow." He got up to turn down the covers.

"What?" Her eyebrows arched in shock. "Seriously?"

"Yes, just because we're in Greece doesn't mean training stops."

"You're such a slave driver."

"I am not." He chuckled. It's my job..."

"Yes, Terminator. I know." She mocked him.

It was one of the first times she'd seen Eli give a full belly laugh. His laughter tickled her so much before she knew it they both lay on the bed giggling like children. He pulled her close as their mirth subsided. "We can sleep in, but we still have to train tomorrow."

She smiled into the crook of his neck. "Okay."

***

Thwack! Her staff struck Mathilda's staff and then she backed off. Sweat was dripping into her eye. She swiped it away. It was hot and they'd been sparring for over an hour. All she wanted to do was jump into the pool. Part of her still felt like she was nursing a hangover.

When she woke up this morning, Eli hadn't been next to her. When she saw him at breakfast he said he'd had to talk to Hadrian and Lysander about when they would be able to head to the Temple of Apollo. He also filled them in on what Ulrik shared with him last night. She'd been glad to have a name to put to the face of the mystery woman from her dream and the battlefield. Katana.

After last night, she had to remember they had a purpose here. She'd read some of her mother's letters this morning to remind her of the importance of finding that book.

A sharp pain coursed down her arm after Mathilda landed a blow because she lost focus.

Get your head back in this or you're going to end up battered and bruised.

She charged at Mathilda and their staffs clashed once more.

"Come on. You had fun last night, but now it's time to get serious." Eli's voice called out to them.

"If I recall, I wasn't the only one who had fun last night." She gave him a knowing look as she remembered how many different ways they'd enjoyed each other's bodies last night.

Eli cleared his throat and crossed his arms over his chest, trying to appear authoritative. Max and Phaedra smirked at him.

She was feeling victorious over having the last word when her feet were knocked out from under her and she saw nothing but sky before her back hit the ground with a thud. A low groan left her mouth while she lay there and recovered.

Thirty seconds later, Eli was standing over her with his hands on his knees. He wasn't even trying to hide his grin.

"Looks like you could use a little help." He reached out his hand to help her up and she swatted it away and sat up.

She had to pay attention with Mathilda. If you took your eyes off that girl for a second you were a goner. Slowly, she rose to her feet.

"Max and Phaedra, why don't you guys go a round." He tossed Willow's staff to Phaedra.

"Wait... but, I'm not..." Willow winced.

"Yes, you are. It's time for a break." She tried to slap him away again, but he wouldn't let her push him away. Once she relented, he helped her over to a lounge chair. "You okay?" He crouched in front of her with her hands in his. She could feel the calluses on his palms from where he handled the staff frequently.

She looked into his eyes. "I'm okay." It was stupid and petty to be upset with him because Mathilda bested her as usual. "What did they say when you talked to them this morning?"

"Hadrian reminded me that the Pythian Games were going on for the next four days and that you were expected to be Mistress of Ceremonies."

She sighed. "I completely forgot about that. My brain is a little foggy after last night."

"We'll be able to begin our search the day after the games are completed." She could tell he was slightly irritated over having to wait that long, but he gave her a smile anyway. She leaned down and hugged him. If she was honest, she was anxious herself. Five days might not feel like torture if she had the Pythian Games to occupy her. Then they would be one more step towards finding the book. It put her mind at ease. Everyday she wanted it to be the end of this thing between her and Killian. It wouldn't fully be over until one of them was dead. Preferably him.

He pulled away. "Why don't we go into town? Have a look around."

"I thought you said we had to train?" She eyed him suspiciously.

"I know what I said, but just for a few hours we'll take a break. Then you and I can come back and meditate, work on Oracle training since Mathilda just beat the shit out of you." He chuckled.

"You asshole." She giggled while she smacked him on his arms. He defended himself against her attack.

"Hey guys. Let's head into town." He called out to the rest of the group.

Willow was so thankful she didn't have to spar the rest of the day.

CHAPTER 6

Eli

WALKING AROUND THE picturesque village of Chrissó was a nice way to spend the afternoon. The narrow cobblestone streets lined with neoclassical architecture provided a romantic setting. Today, he actually felt like just a normal couple, a normal couple out sightseeing. He'd shucked off the role of Protector for a few hours to be a boyfriend. They held hands, talked, laughed. It had been a relaxing day.

The rest of the team was somewhere around the city, but he didn't care. He was enjoying it just being the two of them. They strolled to the village square to grab coffee at a little café they passed earlier.

Willow had removed her shades and leaned back in her chair to soak up the sun. He enjoyed watching her live life without the weight of Killian on her shoulders.

"It's so beautiful here." She sighed and looked over at him. Before he could respond, the waitress delivered their cappuccinos.

"I think you're very beautiful." It may have sounded cheesy and she'd probably tell him so, but he meant it with his whole heart.

She gave him a radiant smile before she leaned across the table and kissed him.

It was the perfect day he mused right before his eyes landed on a familiar face. He blinked twice, hoping his eyes were deceiving him, but no, there she was in the flesh. Katana. They hadn't even gotten to enjoy their coffee. His head whipped around the square and he saw some of her punks coming in from the other side.

'WE'RE IN TROUBLE. GET YOUR ASSES HERE NOW. WE'RE IN THE VILLAGE SQUARE. KATANA'S HERE.' He sent the message telepathically to the group. The square was packed with locals, tourists, families, but he knew Katana didn't care. They were all collateral damage to her. He took one last look at Willow's serene face and wished they had more time, wished she had more time to enjoy what had been a perfect day. "Get under the table."

The minute the words were out of his mouth she froze, the coffee mug poised at her lips. Her eyes registered her panic. She did her best to control her fear but her hand shook when she returned the cup back to the saucer, sloshing some of the hot liquid onto the table. "What's wrong?" Her eyes darted around the square trying to locate the threat. It only took seconds for her eyes to find Katana.

When she looked back at him he remained calm. "The team will be here in a matter of seconds..." Right after he said the words Phaedra and Max appeared in the open seats at the table.

So much for keeping a low profile and trying to keep our magic under wraps.

Out of the corner of his eye, he saw a few of the startled onlookers gawking at their newly arrived tablemates.

"Where is she?" Phaedra asked while scanning the crowd.

"Your three o'clock. I'm pretty sure she knows we've spotted her. Where are the others?"

"They should be searching the perimeter." Her eyes found Katana as she answered Eli's question.

"Get under the table, Willow."

"But, I can help." She pleaded.

Now was not the time for this. She needed to listen to him. "Remember what I said about others not learning about your fae ability right now?" He reminded her, hoping she would listen.

The defiant look didn't leave her face, but she gave him a silent nod and reluctantly slipped underneath the table.

"Do your best to save any innocents. I wouldn't put it past her to use any of these people as shields or ways to distract us. I'm going to stay here." He peeked beneath the table. "Did you bring your dagger with you?" She slipped it from her purse. "Have it ready, just in case."

When he sat back up Phaedra looked at him. "It would be much safer if you teleported Willow back to the villa. You can't teleport within the walls, but you should be able to appear on the front lawn. Take her and go and we'll meet up with you once we deal with them."

Max nodded in agreement.

"Okay. Be safe." He reached beneath the table. "Give me your hand." Willow put her hand in his and they disappeared. When they reappeared they stood at the end of the driveway leading to the villa. Arsenio's car skidded to a halt mere inches from hitting them. Eli wrapped his body around Willow and put himself between her and the vehicle.

"We nearly killed you." Arsenio pulled his huge frame from the passenger seat. "What's happened? Why didn't you come back with the car and driver?"

He uncurled his body from around hers and looked at Arsenio. "The vampires showed up. They were ready to ambush us in the square. Phaedra and the others are still there, dealing with them."

Arsenio's face took on a menacing look. For once, his facial expression matched his intimidating stature. "I'll grab others. We'll provide back up for your friends. Get inside." Arsenio moved with a speed he wasn't aware the man was capable of and opened the door before he went back to the car, the whole time speaking Greek into his phone.

As they entered the front door he looked back over his shoulder at Arsenio's car speeding down the road.

Inside, they didn't stop until they reached the sanctity of the suite that had been assigned to them. After he shut the door, she collapsed onto the bed. "I wasn't stupid enough to think that Killian didn't know where to look for the book. I just thought we'd have time." She said to her lap. "I could have fought, you know." This time she looked at him when she said that statement.

"I know, babe." He walked over and sunk to his knees before her, resting his arms on either side of her on the bed. "I know you're more than capable." He was in no way trying to patronize her or condescend to her. He sighed. "We try not to use our magic in front of humans unless we absolutely have to. There were a lot of humans out there today that would have witnessed our magic and it isn't going to help at all if any of them get caught in the crossfire or worse." He let what he said sink in.

Recognition crossed her face. "You're referring to the anti-supernatural groups that Samson spoke about?"

"Yeah, and it doesn't help that after what Ulrik told me last night, there may be an anti-hybrid group within the supernatural community that I have to worry about too." He pushed up from his leaning position and cupped her face with both hands. "Babe, being part fae makes you a hybrid... and if anything ever happen to you because some idiot gets it in their head they don't like that... I'm not sure what I'd do."

She reached up and rubbed the back of his hand.

"When I ask you to stay out of the fight, I'm not trying to be a jerk. I know you can handle yourself. It's just... I want you safe." It was hard not to relive how close she'd come to death in his mind. He pressed his forehead against hers and shut his eyes.

"Okay."

The fear in his gut unknotted itself, but it wasn't completely gone. He knew Phaedra could more than take care of herself, but he worried about her and everyone else as well. They were his family.

For the next thirty minutes, they sat together on the couch in the living room, waiting for the rest of the Protectors to return. When the front door opened, they both stood up. Anxious looks marked their faces as they waited for people to enter the room. The first one inside was Mathilda. Willow ran to her and wrapped her in a hug. One by one, they each entered the living room. Once he'd seen each of their faces and that they were unharmed, he breathed a sigh of relief. They'd all made it back alive. Lysander, Hadrian, Arsenio, Ulrik and some of the witches from Hadrian's coven he hadn't met yet entered behind them.

"I don't think we can wait another twenty-four hours before going to the ruins." He addressed Hadrian.

"You're right, but with the Pythian Games tomorrow everyone will be expecting Willow. If she's not there it will draw suspicion. She must preside over the Opening Ceremony."

Eli knew he was right, but it didn't mean he liked it. Hadrian continued talking before he could process this information.

"The other problem becomes that the first day of games are scheduled to take place at the theatre and stadium which is near the ruins. The space will not be completely empty like it would have been if we waited until the games are over." Hadrian shared a look with Lysander.

Eli was about to protest when Hadrian put his hands up. "I know we cannot wait. I only tell you this so you are aware of the dangers with so many eyes watching us. If Katana and her gang show up, they will have more people to harm in trying to take what they came for."

There was never going to be an easy way to this. He was thankful he hadn't deluded himself. Yes, they would have preferred for them to hold off, but five days at this point was impossible. Katana would surely have the book by then. They couldn't wait. "What do we need to do to be ready to search the Temple once she finishes her duties at the games?" He asked Hadrian, but his gaze swung to Lysander to gauge his reaction to all of this. Lysander's face was a blank mask.

Hadrian let out a sigh, that reminded Eli how old he was despite his appearance. "I will make the preparations." He left the room with Lysander, Arsenio and the other members of his coven on his heels.

Ulrik approached. "I'm sorry to hear about what happened, but very glad all of you are okay. If I'm not intruding, I'd like to accompany you tomorrow, to be of service if needed, my friend."

Their talk last night killed most of his suspicions about Ulrik's intents and motives and right now they could use all the help they could get. He'd only seen a few vampires with Katana in the square, but that didn't mean there weren't more. "We'd be glad to have you."

Ulrik smiled at him and patted him on the shoulder.

"You heard the man, everyone. We first have to get through the Opening Ceremony and then we'll slip away to head to the Temple. Get some rest. We have an early start and I'm sure it's going to be a long day tomorrow. We'll need to be on guard from any more attacks from Katana." He pulled Phaedra aside for a quick powwow. "What happened in the square?"

"Nothing really. We fought, no casualties on either side. Once Arsenio and his people showed up, she retreated. Ulrik and Arsenio split up the humans afterwards and Ulrik used his powers of persuasion to make them forget and Arsenio cast a spell over the rest to erase their memory of what they saw."

"Glad you're okay."

"You expected a different outcome?" She scowled at him, which made a small smile appear.

"Nope. Knew I'd see you back here."

He watched her walk away. Max grabbed her hand and they headed off to their bungalow. Eli checked on Morgana, Mathilda and Zoriana before he allowed himself to seek out Willow. He found her in the bedroom. She lay on her stomach facing away from him. Before he could say anything, she spoke.

"I don't want anyone getting hurt because of me." The sound was kind of muffled because her face was half buried in her pillow.

He came closer. "What?"

She sat up and faced him, still clutching the pillow she'd just been laying on. "I don't want anyone getting hurt because of me." She looked at her lap with a forlorn expression. He sat on the bed next to her.

"Each of us is prepared to die for you if that's what it takes. It's what we signed up for."

"Why would you sign up to risk your life for some stranger?" Her fingers plucked at the feathers fighting their way out of the goose down pillow in her arms.

"Willow, you're not a stranger." He pulled her into his arms.

"I was when you started out." When her eyes searched his face looking for an answer for why he'd risk everything for a woman he didn't know, his heart went out to her. After her mother's death, there had been no one in her life that cared for her on that level. The idea that someone would willingly put their life on the line for someone else's was hard for her to accept.

"You could ask the same of Secret Service agents that put their life on the line for people like the President on a daily basis. It's part of the job." He lifted her chin so she was looking at him. "But you're more than a job to any of us. I hope you know that."

She didn't say anything. Tears spiked her lashes. He knew it weighed heavily on her shoulders, the thought that one of their lives could be taken so hers would be spared. It was a weighty responsibility and it spoke a lot about her character that she didn't take it lightly. He wanted to comfort her, and tell her she didn't need to feel that way, but doing so would be asking her to change who she was and he wouldn't do that. It made him fall in love with her even more. He kissed her brow. "Let's get some sleep. We have a long day ahead of us."

When she crawled beneath the covers he hoped the dark thoughts that plagued her wouldn't turn into nightmares. He pulled her close; glad she didn't resist him. The idealistic hope that tomorrow would pass without an incident was a fleeting thought. He knew better. Something was surely not going to go according to plan his gut told him.

CHAPTER 7

Willow

IT WAS STILL dark outside and she couldn't stop yawning. Last night, she tossed and turned, worried over what today would bring, that someone might be hurt. It was a miracle she wasn't haunted by Katana or Killian.

Sunrise had yet to crest over the tops of Mount Parnassus. She snuggled next to Eli, her eyes heavy with drowsiness.

"Go to sleep. I'll wake you when we get there." He whispered.

Without another thought she drifted off. She didn't even get out a thank you before she fell into a deep slumber. It felt like only seconds later he was shaking her awake.

"We're here."

The sky was finally starting to get some color as shades of lavender and purple colored the horizon waiting for the sun to begin its ascent. She yawned and stretched before exiting the car. They'd pulled off into a large dirt clearing that seemed to be a makeshift parking lot. She was the only one dressed up for the Opening Day. Thankfully, she'd stuffed a change of clothes in a bag before they left the house.

On any other day, she would have been thrilled to be wearing the designer dress, but today she could muster no excitement over fashion. The shiver that ran through her body wasn't just from the chilly morning air and her lack of proper clothing. She hated to admit, she was a little afraid.

Everyone else wore hiking clothes, prepared for what would come after, when they were able to slip away from the games. The only other person not dressed for a scavenger hunt was Hadrian, who was Master of Ceremonies. He would stay behind at the games to ensure things ran smoothly. The beige summer suit he wore showed he was better suited to that kind of thing than what would come later in the day. When she looked in Lysander's direction, he was rummaging in his backpack. The difference in personality had been the only way for her to tell the twin brothers apart. She focused back on why they were here at this hour.

They'd gathered early near the location of the ruins that housed not only the Temple, but the stadium, Hippodrome, theatre, gymnasium and other ancient sites, along with the Delphi Archaeological Museum, so they could plan before the crowds started to arrive.

Once she was fully awake and they moved closer to the ruins, the feeling she had when she first arrived in Greece, returned with a vengeance. Something was calling to her. Not necessarily calling her name, but calling to her spirit. Was it the ruins? Her ancestors? This land? She wasn't sure. Her head turned this way and that, looking for something. A sign? She wasn't sure what she was searching for.

"You okay?" Eli bent and whispered in her ear.

"Yeah." She was sure he heard the distracted tone in her voice as she continued to look around. Eventually, she gave up and allowed herself to be carried by the crowd that grew around them the closer they got to the theatre.

You couldn't help but marvel at the ancient ruin that had withstood time, man and weather. She wondered what the arena must have looked like in its heyday as people filed in and filled the stone seats. Knowing the hunt they were on to locate The Book of Prophecy, kept her from really enjoying the experience.

Hadrian helped her onto a large, flat stone slab that was being used as the stage. Only the two of them had entered the theatre. The Protectors and the others that would accompany her to the Temple of Apollo opted to wait outside. Everyone was concerned a large group leaving at the same time, right at the start of the games would draw suspicion.

"You look lovely." Hadrian's compliment helped relax her only slightly.

"Thank you." She swallowed and looked out at the mass of people. Damaris and Nyssa sat in the front row. Nyssa waved to her like a crazy person. An easy smile broke out across her face. She was thankful for the woman's enthusiasm. Damaris gave her a demure wave. She waved to the two of them.

Crowds had never made her nervous before. It wasn't so much the crowd that made her nervous, but what was to come once she stepped off this stage. She shifted from foot to foot while she waited for the noise level to die down. It was shocking that thousands of people could grow that silent, but you literally could have heard a pin drop. She cleared her throat. Once again there was no microphone. Hadrian told her the stage had already been endowed with the spell he'd used to amplify her singing the other night. "Ladies and gentleman..." She forced a weak smile. "I'm honored to be your Mistress of Ceremonies tonight and kick off this year's Pythian Games."

Everyone cheered and clapped. This time the smile she wore was genuine. She was humbled by their praise, even if it had more to do with the fact that she was the Oracle. "Thank you." The noise died down once again. "To all of the participants over the next few days, I applaud you for your bravery, skill and heart. Remember to be honorable and above all have fun. I wish you all the best... Let the games begin." She threw her arms into the air. When the crowd went wild once more she mused over where her words had come from. She'd been nervous and unprepared. Clearly, there was something to be said about speaking from the heart.

Hadrian escorted her from the stage while men dressed in Greek warrior costumes marched into the center of the theatre to perform the ancient Pyrrhic War Dance.

She breathed a sigh of relief as she exited the theatre and laid eyes on Eli and the other Protectors. "I'd really like to change before we head to the Temple." She stepped away from the group with Morgana and Mathilda so they could shield her from prying eyes while she changed into some black skinny jeans, a black tank top and some boots. She tucked her dagger into her waistband. Once she finished they rejoined the group. They had about a half-mile walk to the first set of ruins, The Tholos.

It was difficult not to stumble over the rocky terrain in her haste to reach the location. The closer they got, the more she felt some invisible force pulling her towards it.

"Slow down or you're going to hurt yourself." Eli grabbed her by her elbow when she almost took another tumble. "This place has been here for over a thousand years, it's not going anywhere."

She slowed her steps to appease him, but she felt a yearning with every step. Once they passed the Castalian Spring she could see the remaining three Doric columns that made up The Tholos. The sight took her breath away. Even though it was now just ruins, she found it beautiful. She was sure the circular temple that once stood here was magnificent.

Mom, I'm here.

The sense of connectedness she felt to her mother in this place washed over her. For a minute, she just stood there and took it in. It felt like her mother was standing beside her. She blinked back a tear.

Eli came up beside her, breaking the spell. "In your mother's letters does she say anything about where we might find the book?"

"I actually haven't finished reading all of them, but so far she's made no mention of the location of the book." She felt a little ashamed that she'd been hording the letters like some miser and hadn't finished reading them. As much as she wanted to hold onto and savor the letters she realized that the information they contained could help them. "I'm sorry." She looked at Eli.

"It's okay." He put his arm around her and kissed her forehead. "Let's go down and have a look around."

Everyone walked down to the ruins, doing their best to be respectful. No one knew exactly where to search so they fanned out and started looking around.

Mom, what are we looking for?

Was there a trap door, some secret compartment in one of the pillars or was it hidden here by magic? Maybe it was buried at the actual temple?

"Can you use magic to try and detect it? Or conjure it?" She turned hopeful eyes to Eli.

The optimism she hoped to see on his face didn't quite reach his eyes when he smiled at her. "I love the way your mind works... I'd thought of that and I certainly intend to try a locator spell... The thing is, if this book has been hidden away for as long as it has, it wasn't meant to be found or it takes something more than magic to find it."

It was hard not to be disheartened by his words, but she appreciated that he was always truthful with her.

Stepping away from her, he dropped into a crouch. He looked up at her before he shut his eyes. He placed a hand on one of the broken pillars. Latin spilled from his lips in a low voice. One of the last words she heard him utter was, 'reperio.'

Ideally, the book would appear with a pop and fall into her hands, but this wasn't a movie. When Eli fell silent she looked around unsure what she would find or see. Was the ground supposed to glow, shake or spew the book from its depths? Of course, it never was that easy.

When their eyes met he shook his head at her in apology. He'd told her it wouldn't be that easy. "We tried right?" She offered before she turned away and began picking her way through the ruins. Everyone had their heads down, looking among the stones and weeds for some sign, something that would tell them if they were even looking in the right place. After twenty minutes, she found herself near the three remaining columns. She looked up at the pillars and admired them again.

In her mind, something prodded her to touch the column. She wasn't sure where it had come from, because the thought hadn't been there a moment ago. The closer she walked the stronger the urge became to reach out and touch the structure. Her pulse quickened and she swallowed and stepped forward with her hand outstretched. Even though this urge propelled her forward, her steps became slow and uncertain. What would happen when she touched it? She looked up at the top once more before she placed her hand against the sun-warmed stone.

The minute she touched it, that inner voice she'd only heard one other time before said, 'Show me.' Her eyes rolled back into her head and she fell into a trance.

She expected to be shown glimpses of the future, but she saw something else instead... she saw her mother. For a moment, she felt jerked off balance at seeing her dead mother. She thought she could only see the future. So many thoughts about her abilities were manifesting in her head, but she refocused her attention back on her mother.

There her mom stood, in ripped blue jeans and a white peasant blouse, gazing up at the columns the same way she had been. Looking at her, she realized how young her mother was when she died. She was beautiful.

Willow found herself looking around. From the things her mother said in her letters, she hadn't come here alone. That's when she saw a younger looking Hadrian staring at her mother. The only reason she knew it was Hadrian and not Lysander was because of the smile he wore. She had yet to see Lysander crack a smile at all. He walked over and put his arms around her. She leaned into him and he whispered something into her ear and they both laughed. The scene looked so carefree, like two lovers out sightseeing and enjoying a summer day. In all the letters she'd read so far her mother never mentioned a love affair with one of the leaders of the Greek coven.

She spun around and kissed him. When she pulled away, she could see the genuine happiness on her mother's face. Even Hadrian looked giddy. He took her hand and they walked off.

The scene of the two lovebirds dissolved and the ground shook slightly. Elements seemed to swirl, change, shift and move around her. The air whipped and cracked, similar to loud claps of thunder and lightening.

The columns that were once discolored, crumbling and aged were being restored to their former glory and the circular building began to be rebuilt. Her mouth dropped open in surprise when she realized she was going back even further in time to ancient Delphi. In a matter of seconds, when the elements stopped moving, the ruins were reconstructed and she stood in fourth century Greece.

In the brief fashion lesson she'd requested from the women that dressed her the night of the Bacchanalia, she knew the men were dressed in chitons made of light linen and the women wore peplos made of heavier wool but draped, fashioned and decorated with brooches and pins. The male and female tunics and garments were dyed vibrant shades and colors. Some of the people wore sandals while quite a few walked barefoot.

It should have been impossible, but from her vantage point she suddenly had a bird's eye view of everything: the splendor that once made up the thriving metropolis of Delphi. The Sacred Way zigzagged its way through the Sanctuary of Apollo. The Treasury of the Athenians was now whole. She wondered at the treasures and riches it would have held in this era. The theatre was even more spectacular than it was earlier when she'd opened up the Pythian Games. The pools of the gymnasium sparkled and glistened as people frolicked in the water. Athletic statues dotted many areas, paying homage to the feats and strengths of many brave souls.

When she returned her attention to The Tholos and looked through the doorway of the vaulted temple she could see pilasters that jutted from the wall and rested on a stone bench. She took a few steps back and looked up at the dome of the circular temple. It was covered in intricate decoration and depictions of Centaurs in battle. It was amazing to see the structure intact and pristine.

She turned her attention back to the people. Everyone seemed to be heading to the larger temple that sat another half a mile away. Using her hand as a shield from the sun, she was able to get a better glimpse of the Temple of Apollo. She began to walk in that direction when she heard her name being called and suddenly she was jolted back into the present.

She blinked. Eli stood in front of her.

"What did you see?" He looked at her anxiously.

"Nothing that could help us... I didn't see the future." She looked at his confused expression. "I saw the past... I saw my mother."

"Retrocognition?"

"What?"

"That's what it's called, the ability to see the past. I'd been doing more research on your Oracle abilities, trying to learn what else you might be capable of. I wasn't sure if you would be able to or not. It could be a good thing."

"I don't think I have any control over it... it only seemed to happen because something was telling me to touch the column. The minute I did, it showed me my mother. She was here." Willow looked towards the Temple of Apollo ruins. "I think we need to head there. In my vision, I was walking towards it before I heard your voice..." She turned back to Eli. "I think we'll find our answers there." She was sure he wanted to know what she was shown of the past, but there would be time for that later. Right now, she just wanted to get to the other ruins.

He didn't push for answers. "Let's head over to The Temple of Apollo everyone. Willow believes we'll find what we're looking for over there."

They ended their search of The Tholos and began the hike towards the main ruins. In the distance, the rumble of the spectators in the theatre could be heard and she wondered what was taking place at this moment.

CHAPTER 8

Eli

HE COULDN'T HELP wondering what the past revealed to her. Either she was still processing it or she didn't want to talk about it. He did his best to never push her before she was ready to share. They walked side by side and it was clear she was lost in replaying whatever it was she saw.

These ruins covered a larger area than The Tholos. Once they reached the temple's ruins, he stooped and placed his hand on one of the decaying pillars. "Indica mihi quem quaerimus. Reperio." He waited. Nothing.

Magic was not going to be what unearthed The Book of Prophecy; that was clear to him now. He stood and dusted his hands on his jeans. When his eyes met hers he shook his head. She tried to give him a smile, which seemed more like a grimace before she turned away and wandered around.

He knew she wanted this all to just be over. He did to. Some of the others tried to cast spells to locate the book with the same results. Nothing. Phaedra walked towards him.

"Anything?" She must have figured Willow had a clue or something that would help.

"No."

She looked out at the mountains. "It's like looking for a needle in a haystack, but not know which haystack to look in." The exasperation in her voice was evident. He felt it too.

Why did her mother tell her about the existence of the book, but not where or how to find it? Unlike the ruins of The Tholos that were almost picturesque, the ruins of the Temple of Apollo weren't much to look at. Here there only remained six jagged columns of varying heights, which stood taller than anything else. The rest of the ruins just consisted of the foundation of what once was a temple people traveled to from all over to visit, and hear the mighty Oracle speak.

A quick flash in his mind showed Willow much the same way she looked the other night in her toga, giving prophecies and visions to the generals and emperors that came to have their destinies revealed to them.

His boot kicked at a few pebbles as he watched Willow walk over to the columns. She had her back to him, her hands wrapped around her torso, almost like she was hugging herself. There was no way she could be cold out here. It was blazing hot. Before he could give it any more thought, the ground rumbled and shook. Then the earth began to fracture, like an earthquake was tearing it apart from the inside. He stumbled around, as did everyone else, trying to find something to hold onto and keep their balance. Out of the corner of his eye he could see some people had been knocked to the ground by the force of the quake.

"Willow!" She was right near a portion of the fragmented ground. She wasn't looking at him, but she looked terrified. The uneven, shaky ground had her swaying. She'd dropped into a crouch to try and steady herself. There was no way for him to get to her. A vapor or mist rose from the fissures where she stood. Icy fingers wrapped themselves around his heart. What if the gas was poisonous and she breathed it in. "Willow! Cover your mouth!" He tried to yell above the rumbling of the earth that quaked beneath their feet.

Thankfully, she heard him. She covered her mouth and watched with wide, fearful eyes as the vapor rose around her. Seconds later, he saw her hands drop to her sides and her body go rigid, before she fell to the ground convulsing.

Fuck!

Fear, adrenaline and anger coursed through his veins. Agony sunk its teeth into his guts and tore them to ribbons as he watched her writhe on the ground. Was the gas killing her? She wasn't screaming. Was it because the mystery gas was choking her to death? He attempted to use his magic to try and stop the earthquake. When that didn't work, he tried to use magic to end whatever was happening to her. Again, nothing. Whatever had caused the earthquake and vapors had also quelled his magic. He was reminded of how helpless he felt on the battlefield watching that spear run through her body.

A frustrated roar erupted from his throat.

Not again.

He would not stand by and watch her suffer again. Even if it meant his life, he would get to her. It was like God or something in the universe heard him, because the ground stilled. The gaseous substance continued to flow from the crevices the earth had cut open around Willow.

Lysander somehow beat him over to her body, but he only came within fifteen or twenty feet of her and didn't go any further. Eli was about to run past him to get to Willow when Lysander blocked him. "Don't touch her." His voice was calm. "Not when she's like that."

Despite Lysander's demeanor, he was anything but calm. He pushed against him. No one and nothing would keep him from saving Willow. "Let me go. She needs me.

Look at her." He shoved against Lysander again. If he had to put this man flat on his ass he would, especially if he didn't move out of his way.

"I have looked at her and I'm telling you she doesn't need you. She's not hurt and she's not in pain."

He'd had enough. If Lysander wanted a fight, he was about to get one. Usually, he could keep a cool head, but when it came to her, he wouldn't stand by and let something happen to her if there was something he could do about it. "If you don't step out of my way, I won't apologize for what I do next." He was ready to use magic to remove Lysander from his path if needed. At this point, everyone had formed around them. He could see Phaedra gearing up for a brawl if it came to that. The other Protectors also looked ready to have his back.

"Look at her eyes." Lysander didn't seem fazed one bit by the fact that anger seeped out of every pore or that Eli was close to laying hands on him or worse. "Look." He said the word more forcefully this time.

Eli's chest rose and fell with agitation, but reluctantly he let his gaze drift to Willow. Lysander continued to restrain him.

Willow's eyes had gone a glassy white like they did back at the Walker coven during their last training there, a milky white like he'd just seen at The Tholos ruins when she saw the past. Lysander was right. She wasn't injured... Willow was seeing the future. His body relaxed and he took a step back.

"The Pythia, the original Oracle of Delphi, Willow's ancestors saw some of her visions this way. It was not uncommon. It's not pretty to watch..." He looked over his shoulder at the jerking movements of Willow's body and limbs and turned back to Eli. "We have to let it take its course. These ruins, this place..." He looked around and up at the sky. "It must have recognized who she was. The Temple of Apollo may no longer stand, but the ancestors know one of their own. This place is still imbued with power."

Eli could only hope that not only was she seeing the future, hopefully she was getting a glimpse on where to find the book.

As Willow continued in her trance, Arsenio spoke up. "I've tried to call Hadrian to see if they experienced the earthquake, but I've gotten no response. Maybe I should send some of the men back to make sure everything is all right at the theatre."

"Good idea." Lysander threw over his shoulder.

Arsenio pulled two men from the group and gave them instructions. They disappeared into thin air.

Even though he was aware that Willow was in no danger, it didn't take away his worry or concern. This was still new to her and it was the longest she'd been under. He crossed his arms over his chest and waited.

Morgana came up on one side and Mathilda on his other side. Mathilda put her arm around him. "She's okay." Her young voice sounded so strong and sure that it gave him confidence that it was the truth.

"I know you worry about her, but she's strong. She's a fighter, that one." Morgana echoed Mathilda's reassurances.

He appreciated having them here. It wasn't easy caring about someone as deeply as he cared for Willow. She'd told him she could take care of herself and he knew that, but it didn't stop him from wanting to take care of her as well.

CHAPTER 9

Willow

THE MINUTE THE ground started shaking fear seized her insides. She couldn't reach out for Eli because a large crack had broken across the ground before she could move. It wasn't that wide, but with the way the ground rolled beneath her feet she could have lost her footing trying to jump across and plunged to her death. She had no idea how deep the chasm was that opened and she wasn't going to find out.

She couldn't have explained it later when asked, but the fear left her body and then it felt like she was no longer in control of herself when her body went completely still. It wasn't exactly an out of body experience, but for a moment she no longer even felt the ground tremble, and then in the next instant her limbs and body were flailing about of their own volition. In medical terms, they would have said she had a seizure. The thing was, it didn't hurt. Her limbs and head thrashed around, beat against the ground, but there was no pain.

The first vision she saw began with thunder cracking and lightening flashing across a red sky. When she looked around she stood outside a dense, thicket of trees and on the other side of her was a castle. It seemed familiar to her, but she couldn't exactly place why. She looked up at the sky and noticed that a total solar eclipse was happening. Shouldn't that have made the sky go black?

What's causing the red color?

The air smelled damp and redolent with the sickly sweet odor of... death. In the instant that another thunderclap sounded she knew this was Killian's castle.

Where is this?

She looked this way and that, searching for an answer like she would suddenly see a sign that would alert her to the location. Before she could do any investigating the vision started to disintegrate the same way it did earlier.

No, no, no.

If only there was a way to control the vision, so she could stay in it long enough to get more information. She wanted to stomp her foot like a child. When elements stopped swirling she found herself in utter blackness. It frightened her at first and then she heard a heartbeat. The rhythm wasn't normal though, the thump thump she heard beat twice as fast as hers. Then she saw it. It was like someone was using a camera and zooming out: a tiny foot, a leg, ribcage, a tiny hand with little fingers that twitched slightly and then a translucent eyelid where the veins were visible... a baby, a baby that was still inside its mother's womb. She was hearing a fetal heartbeat. The baby seemed backlit by a light, the way she was able to see the organs. It was clear the baby was still growing. It was a marvel to get to see this stage of its development.

Whose baby am I seeing?

She noticed something spark next to the child. Maybe it was just her eyes. What was that? She was about to blink when the spark happened again and lasted a moment longer than it did before and then cut out.

What is that? Is that normal?

She was so intrigued by being able to see life at this early stage, the spark was forgotten when her eyes went back to the baby.

After a few more moments, the elements shifted and moved around and the scene was gone. She was beginning to grow used to it now.

This time she found herself in a large, dimly lit room that looked like something out of the United Nations. Around the room, rows and rows of chairs sat behind desks and there were placards and name tags that sat in front of each chair. She walked over to the nearest desk and picked up the name plate. Where you might see a name and a country if this was the United Nations, instead it said a name and supernatural faction underneath. The one she picked up read Aine Sparklefrost, Faery.

What an interesting sounding name.

Seeing the word faery made her think of her lineage, her father. Would this Aine person know him?

Out of the corner of her eye she saw some shadows being cast against the wall and when she looked over at them she could see a few people huddled in a corner of the room. Although she couldn't hear anything, she had the sneaking suspicion that the meeting was a secret one from the way they leaned in to whisper and they kept looking around like they were afraid of being caught. Since the light was too low she couldn't make out anything. What if they were plotting to do something evil? She tried to race down to the front to see their faces, but the elements began to swirl and shift.

Come on.

Every single time, it seemed to take her out of the vision at the most inopportune time.

In the next vision she saw herself in a room with Zoriana. She was looking at their backs. It felt like they were at the Walker coven, but she couldn't be sure. She'd never been in the room before. Only candlelight lit the room. Whatever they were doing it appeared that they didn't want to be caught doing it. They were huddled over a book.

What if it's...

She rushed over to try and peer over Zoriana's shoulder, but it was like a cord or something was tethered to her back. It yanked her back from the scene. She reached out trying to clutch onto it and hold it, grab it back, but the further she was pulled the smaller the scene became until she was in the blackness again. It felt like she was falling. She tried to reach up and grab a hold of something in the nothingness, but there was nothing to grab a hold of. Wherever she was started coming into focus and it stopped feeling like her body was hurtling to its death. Now it felt like she was falling in slow motion the way her limbs floated above her. Within seconds, she landed softly on her back on a limestone floor. She stared up at the ceiling for a second, trying to acclimate to her environment before she sat up.

Once she sat up, she looked around and saw statues of many Greek gods and then a huge hearth. As she completed her 360-degree view of the place her eyes landed on a woman sitting atop a chair that looked like it was on stilts. This woman was no statue. She was flesh and blood. The sight of her startled Willow and she found herself scuttling backwards in a crab-like walk trying to get away. Had the woman been there the whole time.

When the woman didn't come down from the chair or seem to pose some sort of threat, she stopped moving. The woman looked at her with curious, but knowing, hazel colored eyes.

"Where am I?"

"You don't know?" Her voice had a wise, otherworldly quality. Willow took in the way she was dressed. She wore the ancient Grecian dress, the peplos, she'd seen women wearing in her earlier vision. The material had been dyed a maroon or burgundy, she wasn't quite sure in the inadequate light. The garment was draped and fastened with a few ornamental pins and buttons. The loose fitting veil didn't entirely cover her long, wavy chestnut hair. Her tawny beige skin had a healthy glow.

A sudden movement on the woman's chair revealed a large Python wrapped around the back and arms of the chair. It was moving. Willow gulped.

This was not the future. She was in the past, in ancient Greece once again to be exact.

"You're The Pythia." This time it wasn't a question. She made the statement with conviction. With crystal clear clarity, Willow realized she was speaking with the original Oracle. This woman was her ancestor.

She must have seen her eyeing her pet. "He will not hurt you."

So you say.

That didn't stop her from being afraid of the beast that looked like it was at least ten feet long.

The Pythia didn't seem to have any interest in getting to know her. "You may ask one question. Choose wisely."

Willow licked her suddenly dry lips, her eyes darted back and forth before she swallowed and spoke. "Where is the Book of Prophecy?"

The Pythia smiled a secret smile. "What is the creature that walks on four legs in the morning, two legs at noon and three in the evening?"

Willow's stomach dropped.

Seriously?

The one question she could ask was met with a riddle? Why couldn't anything ever be easy?

"But..."

The Pythia's smile widened and Willow could feel the elements about to shift once more. "Wait. Please..." She tried to request more time, a different answer, anything that would actually help them. It was too late. She had already gone. In the next instant, Willow blinked her eyes a few times and found herself looking at the sky.

Now, where am I?

"Willow?"

When she heard Eli's familiar voice, she raised herself up onto her elbows and turned to look in his direction. She was back in the ruins and everyone stood in a group. The earth no longer shook and the vapor had disappeared.

He rushed over to her and knelt beside her. "You're okay." It was like he was reassuring himself that she was in fact okay. The others crowded around behind him.

"Yeah, I'm okay. A little dazed." She shook her head and then remembered the riddle The Pythia gave her in response to her question on where The Book of Prophecy might be located. "Listen, I saw The Pythia..."

The mouths of the witches from the Greek coven fell open in shock and awe. "What? You saw The Pythia?" They marveled over this.

"Right now isn't the time, but I promise I will share more details later, about her and what the temple looked like. Right now, I need everyone's help in deciphering a riddle she gave me that's supposed to lead us to The Book of Prophecy. I didn't expect her to be so cryptic..."

"Willow, the riddle. What's the riddle?" Phaedra cut her rambling off.

"Sorry. The riddle is, 'What is the creature that walks on four legs in the morning, two legs at noon and three in the evening?'"

Nearly everyone was about to answer when Arsenio tsked her like he'd done in the car when he had to teach her about the Pythian Games. "Not only is your ancient Greek history lacking, but clearly your reading is as well. Most Greeks know that riddle. It is from Sophocles' Oedipus Tyrannus. The Sphinx gives Oedipus the riddle to solve or she will kill him. I believe she will strangle him or eat him or something." Arsenio mused, trying to remember if he was correct or not.

She tried not to linger on the fact that her education must have been severely lacking if she was literally one of the only people in the group that didn't know about the riddle or else she hadn't been paying attention that day in school. Either way they had no time for one of Arsenio's lessons as much as she enjoyed it last time. "Sphinx. The Sphinx. It must mean the book is in Cairo right? Think about it. Cora told me my ancestors were Greeks that married Egyptians. It makes sense that someone would have transported the book to Egypt to keep it safe." She was excited and about to continue her theory when Mathilda spoke.

"What if it's Thebes and not Cairo? Oedipus was traveling to Thebes when he met the Sphinx."

No. In her gut, Willow knew it was Cairo. She didn't get the same feeling of certainty she got when Thebes was uttered.

"No. I'm telling you its Cairo."

Guess The Pythia knew what she was doing the whole time by giving me a riddle that most any Greek would be able to solve.

She sent up a silent prayer of thanks, not sure whether it would reach her or not.

Eli was about to help her up from the ground when in a blur of movement one of the witches from the Castellanos coven had his throat ripped open.

"Vampires!" Someone yelled and then all hell broke loose.

Ulrik moved the quickest out of anyone, dispatching two of the vampires in swift movements that could not be seen by the naked eye. All of the witches went into battle mode, some conjuring weapons out of thin air, others using spells to attack the oncoming vampires. Max morphed into the vicious wolf that belied his witty nature and began to battle some of the bloodsuckers.

Eli helped her to her feet and when she looked up he was about to be attacked. Since his back was turned he would be wounded or killed.

"Look out!" Willow used both hands to blast energy at the vampire that snuck up behind Eli, ready to take him out. She knew what he'd said about people learning about her faery side, but she'd have to deal with that later. There was no way she would sit on her hands for fear of someone learning she was a hybrid, especially if she could protect the people she cared about.

CHAPTER 10

Eli

IT WAS CLEAR the vampires didn't have The Book of prophecy because they were on the wrong continent just like they were. If Katana was as formidable an opponent as Ulrik painted her to be, he was sure they were here to try and take Willow who would ultimately be able to locate the book at this point and then they would eventually have both. They were getting neither.

As much as he would have liked to keep Willow's fae abilities under wraps, there was no way he could. She'd had no choice when she blasted that vampire. This fight called for all hands on deck. The two of them fought back to back.

So far he had yet to see Katana, but he knew she was there, watching and waiting for the right moment, the right opportunity. He was vigilant while he still managed to fend off attacks by her minions she'd sent to tire him out.

Around him, he saw Lysander and Arsenio casting spells that snapped limbs or broke necks and temporarily paralyzed or knocked out some of the vampires. Mathilda and Zoriana fought back to back. He wondered if Mathilda realized. Of course, he knew that no matter how much of a grudge she might be carrying against her mother right now, she always had her back in a fight. Morgana wasn't that far away, engaged in battle with two of the bloodsuckers and holding her own.

Then she was there, looking like a Bond villain, her hair whipping out behind her as she approached him. He'd been looking forward to taking her on solo, but didn't mind when Phaedra positioned herself behind her. Katana looked over her shoulder at her and then back at him. "I guess it won't be just the two of us." She gave him a fake pout. He responded with a deadpan look.

'ENOUGH GAMES.'

Her face took on a lethal look when he communicated with her telepathically.

'I'LL TRY NOT TO STEP ON YOUR CORPSE ON MY WAY OUT OF HERE WITH YOUR GIRLFRIEND.'

They charged one another. He was somewhat surprised she didn't try and use her super speed. It would be to her advantage.

"Terra ortum." He used magic to make the ground rise and move as she ran towards him, hoping to cause her to stumble and fall. No such luck. She simply hovered for a second before flying towards him.

Her focus was so intent on him, she missed Phaedra landing a hit with a flying piece of column from the ruins. It smacked Katana in the side, causing her to fall to the ground. She wasn't injured at all, merely angry. The look she threw Phaedra would have sent most people running, but Phaedra stood her ground and waited to see what Katana would do next.

Eli took this opportunity and pulled a tree out of the ground by its roots using magic so he could use it as a battering ram against her. He got one good lick in before she smashed it to splinters.

Phaedra blasted her with a bolt of electricity, which dropped her to the ground. Eli chanced a glance back at Willow to make sure she was okay. She'd just daggered one of the vampires and then shot a blast of energy at another one, sending them flying backwards.

When he turned back around, Katana had recovered. She was getting back up on her feet. In a quick movement, she picked up a piece of the ruins and hurled it in his direction. He barely managed to dodge the flying piece of debris that would have seriously injured him or knocked him unconscious.

Two vampires began a fight with Phaedra that drew her away from their fight with Katana. He was sure that wasn't a coincidence.

'GUESS YOU DON'T LIKE GETTING YOUR ASS KICKED DO YOU?' He smirked. Of course it pissed Katana off like he knew it would and she came flying in his direction. "Integumentum." He used his magic to turn the air around him into a shield. When Katana hit she bounced off. With Katana's brute strength he knew the shield could probably only take another hit or two before the spell was broken. Katana rammed herself against the air shield once more and he could feel it ready to give way. Before he could cast his next spell something caught Katana's leg and pulled her backwards away from him.

Phaedra had used the air to create an invisible rope, which she now had wrapped around Katana's ankle. She whipped the rope around once and tossed her away. It only gave him a small reprieve to come up with his next move, but he was grateful.

He was about to suggest to Phaedra that they both attack her at once when Katana dropped to her knees and clutched her head in excruciating pain. When he looked around he noticed the other vampires in a similar state. Who was doing that? He turned around and looked at Willow. She shrugged her shoulders. When his eyes scanned everyone again, he saw Morgana in deep concentration. Her nose was bleeding.

It was a lot of magic for one witch to sustain on so many people. Morgana stumbled as she started to weaken.

Beads of sweat broke out on her brow as she strained to stay in control. It was just enough for Katana to break free from the attack and beat a hasty retreat. After that, the other vampires still standing were able to break free and follow Katana. Morgana dropped to her hands and knees exhausted. They rushed to her side. "You okay?" Zoriana asked. She knelt next to her.

He tried to check her over for injuries and when he pulled his hand back it was smeared with blood. "You're hurt."

"It's nothing. A scratch."

"Are you sure?" Lysander asked while trying to get a good look.

Ulrik stepped forward. "I must apologize. I was the one who injured her." Everyone's heads whipped towards him, to stare in disbelief.

"It was my fault. I didn't recognize him in the fight. Friendly fire so to speak." She grimaced when Zoriana pressed a rag to the superficial wound on her arm. "He was only reacting to my attack." She came to his defense.

For a minute, Eli worried if he'd been mistaken in his judgment of Ulrik, but when Morgana confessed to attacking him first, he relaxed. Ulrik was the only vampire on their side. He could understand how in the heat of battle something could happen like that. Morgana would be fine. It wasn't anything serious.

Ulrik had a weird look on his face as he walked away. Eli chalked it up to him feeling badly about injuring Morgana. Zoriana tended to the wound and was able to heal it with no problem. Even though they'd all expended a lot of magic, her wound wasn't serious enough that it required a copious amount of magic to heal it.

"Thank you." Morgana told Zoriana, who helped her stand.

It wasn't until that was dealt with that Eli noticed some of the witches from the Castellanos coven looking at Willow strangely. Then he remembered that they would have seen her use her fae abilities. A nervous feeling settled in his stomach when he recalled Ulrik's words during the banquet about the anti-hybrid hostility some supernaturals were exhibiting. Maybe they'd worn out their welcome. It might be time to head back to Salem and regroup, especially since they could now confirm the book was not here.

"Arsenio. Could we head back to the villa?"

"Of course. I will have the cars waiting for us." He opened up his phone and made a call.

Eli was about to grab Willow and head back to the parking lot when his eye caught a small shiny object in the dust. He walked over and picked it up. It was half of a locket. It was made of gold and oval-shaped. When he turned it some dirt obscured the photo that had been put inside. He used his thumb to wipe it away. Staring back at him was a smiling, carefree Katana with her arms around a man. It was Katana before she'd become a vengeful vampire and Killian's right hand. He pocketed the broken piece of jewelry.

It was hard to think of Katana as once having a heart that cared and loved. Realizing the loss she suffered and the atrocities she'd endured he wondered if he wouldn't have become like her too if Willow had died that day. He pushed the thought to the back of his mind, not wanting to further examine the thin line that separated the two of them. He grabbed Willow and followed the group to the cars.

Back at the house, he assembled the Protectors out in the courtyard. When he was sure they wouldn't be overheard he spoke. "I think it's time for us to head home. We know the book isn't here and..." He wasn't sure whether he should tell them or not.

"What? What is it? Something has you all jumpy." Phaedra narrowed her eyes at him in suspicion.

"Okay listen, during our first night here, I learned about some rumblings in regards to people being anti-hybrid..." Mathilda and Morgana were the only two that looked shocked. The others were old enough and had been around long enough to know that just because you could instantly grow fur, fangs or shoot electricity out of your fingertips, it didn't make people immune to prejudices. "I'd told Willow to lay low with being part fae, but after the fight today when some of them realized she's not just an Oracle... let's just say the tide could turn pretty quick once word starts to spread and I'd rather be on home turf if something goes down. We don't know these people and I'm not sure who exactly would have our back."

Everyone nodded in understanding.

"We leave tomorrow, first thing in the morning." Phaedra looked around at the group, making sure everyone understood that it wasn't up for debate. They were getting the hell out of Greece.

"Get packed up tonight. I'll talk with Arsenio about getting transportation to the train so we can get to Athens." Eli gave the final instructions.

Everyone turned to head to their rooms.

"Guys?" They turned to look at Max. "This might be a little irrelevant given it's not what we need to know in order to locate the book, but I've never read Sophocles. You guys mentioned the Sphinx told Oedipus the riddle, but no one said what the actual answer to the riddle was... What was the answer? I have to know." Max looked around at the other Protectors.

Everyone except Willow said in unison. "Man." Then they turned and walked away shaking their heads.

Max still looked perplexed as he tried to piece together how that worked out. "Oh. I got it." He called out to their retreating backs. "Babe, wait up." He called to Phaedra before running to catch up with her.

Before Eli could head back to the room with Willow, Ulrik stopped him. "If I may speak with you?"

He motioned for Willow to head to the room and he'd join her shortly.

"What's up?"

"I know you're leaving tomorrow. Possibly heading to Egypt to look for the book. I would like to come with you." Nothing came out as a question. Only statements.

"Were you eavesdropping on our conversation?" He stepped closer towards Ulrik and glared at him. Ulrik didn't seem the least bit worried about someone overhearing their conversation or fazed by Eli's change in demeanor.

"No, but like you, I saw the way they looked at her."

Ulrik was way more perceptive than he gave him credit for.

"I understand you want to get her out of here as soon as possible in case there may be trouble. As I told you already, some will have an issue with her being a hybrid. They love and adore her now, but how many will turn their back and perhaps even throw stones later once they know? I could be a big help to you." He made a very persuasive argument and may be one of the few people that knew and had experience with what they might face if things got that bad.

"Yeah, you can come."

A grin broke out on the Dane's face. "Thank you."

"We'll be leaving in the morning. You better be ready. We won't wait."

On his way to the bedroom, he noticed Damaris walking down another hallway. It wasn't that she looked like she was trying not to be seen, but it just seemed strange. Her presence here confirmed that she must be seeing Hadrian. If she was involved with him, then he shouldn't need to worry. It was still unfortunate he'd never had the opportunity to chat with her while they were here. They were leaving first thing in the morning so it didn't matter.

CHAPTER 11

Willow

LATER THAT NIGHT, Willow slipped from the suite. Earlier she'd seen him come down this hallway and could only hope she was going in the right direction. Most people were in bed at this hour and here she was skulking about like an intruder. When she came to the end of the hallway after passing only one other door she figured this had to be it. She knocked on what she hoped was Hadrian's room. With them leaving tomorrow she knew she needed to confront him before they left. After a minute, he answered the door. She could tell he must have hastily thrown on some clothes because the linen shirt he wore was unbuttoned and part of the collar was folded under. The linen pants he'd put on made it obvious he was going commando. Hadrian was pretty well endowed.

Go mom.

She thought, but then quickly realized she was ogling her mother's boyfriend and flushed.

"Willow. Is everything okay?" He peeked behind her and around the corner not hiding his surprise.

"Everything is fine. Maybe I shouldn't have come. I interrupted you. I'm sorry." She turned to leave.

OMG. What if he was in there with Damaris and I just interrupted them? Eli did say he believed they were a couple. That's why he had to throw on clothes because I interrupted them having sex.

She wanted to get away as fast as possible. The way he'd looked at her ever since she arrived had her conjuring up images of him asking her to join them for a threesome. She tried to hurry away.

"Wait." He stepped out of his room and shut the door behind him. In bare feet he padded towards her. He adjusted his collar and buttoned a few of the buttons on his shirt. Maybe he didn't want things to be awkward either.

"Why don't we walk out by the pool?"

She nodded at his suggestion. Outside, they walked the perimeter of the pool. For a while neither of them said anything. "I'm sorry. I knocked on your door in the middle of the night and now I'm not saying anything... I'm not sure how to bring this up." She stopped walking and turned to face him. Before she could stop herself she blurted out what she wanted to know. "Were you my mother's lover?"

Hadrian looked startled.

"I know that question seems to have come from nowhere, but today at the ruins, I had a... a flashback... um, no. Not a flashback because it wasn't my memory." She looked down at the ground rambling, saying that last sentence more to herself than to him. Her eyes looked into his. "At the ruins today, I had a vision of you with my mom. You kissed. It was clear you meant something to each other... I was hoping you would confirm it." She looked at him expectantly and tried not to fidget.

When he sighed and slumped down on one of the lounge chairs, she sat on the one across from him. "I wasn't sure whether you knew or if I should tell you." He finally looked at her. "I cared for her deeply."

"Is that why you looked at me the way you did when we first met? Because I look like her?"

"Yes. It's very hard for me." He peered at her from underneath his lashes.

"I know this might be hard, but this was one of the last places my mother was at before she died... or was possibly murdered." She bit her lip to keep from getting too emotional. "Can you tell me if anything happened here? If she came across anyone that might have been an enemy?"

"No. Everyone liked your mother. I was shocked and devastated when I heard the news." It was hard not to feel disappointment. She wasn't sure what she expected him to say. It wasn't exactly like he was about to hand her a motive and a suspect. There was still nothing that said that it was a murder and not just an accident.

"Thank you." She was about to leave when he spoke again.

"Willow, does anyone else know?" He regarded her with an uneasy look.

She shook her head. "No, I wanted to confirm it with you first."

He took her hand in his and dropped his voice. "Maybe, it should stay our little secret. I don't know if you're aware of this, but there are some supernaturals that don't like the idea of supernaturals from different factions mixing."

Ever since Eli had told her about that, it made her feel sick to her stomach. She scowled and looked at him with sad eyes. "Yeah, I've heard and it fills me full of rage. Why are people such idiots? I would think in the supernatural community that wouldn't matter, but I guess for some people it does." Her face scrunched into a look of displeasure. "Don't worry. I won't say anything. I don't want you to get hurt just for loving my mother..." She placed her free hand over his. "You should know when I saw her in my vision, I could tell she was happy. You made her really happy Hadrian. I'm glad in her final days she had that." She gave him a quick hug and then turned and walked away.

***

To her shock, Lysander had accompanied them to the train station. He was probably ready for them to leave and only making sure they were actually getting on the train. He hadn't said a single word to her since she'd been here. He might look like his brother, but they were nothing alike.

As they pulled up at the station, she noticed the maenads were standing on the curb. Arsenio must have made a call to tell them they were leaving.

Nyssa and Damaris stood in front of her fan club. Damaris was her usual subdued self, but Nyssa looked like she'd already had way too much sugar or caffeine. She half expected them to hold up signs. Nyssa stepped forward with a pout on her face. "We hate that you must leave so soon." The woman ran forward and hugged her and the others followed suit. Pretty soon she was suffocating from the big group hug. When they finally released her she let out a much needed breath.

"Thank you. It's been fun." It was the only thing she could think to say.

Nyssa gave her one last wave and they walked off. Lysander and Arsenio walked up as they walked away.

"It has been lovely to meet you. I do hope we meet again." Arsenio smiled and then wrapped her in a big hug. She was going to miss him.

"It was nice to meet you too, Arsenio."

He proceeded to give each of them a hug. Then Lysander stepped forward. He held his hand out to Eli and they shook hands. "If you need anything further, you know where to find us." After the handshake concluded, his eyes rested on her for a few seconds. He said nothing and his face gave nothing away. Then he turned on his heel and left. She thought his behavior strange and interesting much like the man.

Over twenty-four hours later they were back in the U.S. It felt a little like coming home when they boarded the Protectors RV 2.0 and headed to Salem. Ulrik had been a great travel companion. It was nice to have him along. She knew he'd told Eli things about Killian and Katana. She'd wanted to ask her own questions, but hadn't found the right time. Maybe once they were at the coven. He could possibly have some ideas on how to deal with Killian.

Her thoughts were presently consumed with finding The Book of Prophecy. Now that they knew it was in Egypt, what was there next move going to be. It was a good possibility that they were currently one step ahead of Killian since he would have no clue where the book was located.

They arrived at the Walker house late at night. There was no waiting for Archie to come and greet them this time around since most would be asleep at this hour. All they wanted to do was get to their beds.

When Eli turned around to shut the door, they found Ulrik still standing outside on the porch.

"It's late Ulrik. I know you haven't been on U.S. soil in a while, but we can sightsee another time. It's late." She yawned to indicate just how late. It was hard not to be annoyed that he was keeping her from her bed.

"Yeah, come on man." Eli gestured him inside.

Everyone stared at him, still standing perfectly still on the other side of the door.

Ulrik was amused, judging by the look on his face. "All of you must be very tired if you forgot." He pointed to himself. "Vampire. I cannot come in unless you invite me."

So that was a thing? If only she could disinvite Killian from her dreams.

"Ulrik, you are invited inside. Please come in." Eli said with a mocking bow.

The Dane stepped over the threshold.

"I'll show you to a room." Zoriana smiled tiredly. "Then I'm going to find my husband and sleep." It was the first genuine smile she'd seen on the woman's face in a while, it wasn't the kind of smile that only hid her pain. It was probably a comfort to come home to someone that loved her. She led Ulrik down the hall. Everyone else said their good nights and departed for their rooms.

Last time she was here, she didn't get to see Eli's quarters. A little thrill ran through her at seeing what his space would look like. Unlike the room she inhabited last time she was at the Walker House, Eli's suite was a far contrast.

The living room was painted a light gray with abstract and modern art decorating the walls. A large Chesterfield sofa sat against one wall with a giant flat screen TV mounted on the opposite wall over a cabinet. An Eames lounge chair sat in one corner. There were shelves overflowing with books. The coffee table even had a few books sitting on top. His place was very cozy.

She smiled sleepily at him. "I really like how you decorated it. It feels very... you."

He pulled her close and kissed her forehead before walking further into the room and switching on a lamp. The light illuminated a kitchen sitting off of the living room.

"What? You have a kitchen?" She walked into the room filled with modern, stainless steel appliances.

"You stayed in one of the guest rooms while you were here. If you'd wanted a kitchen we could have added one on for you, but you never said anything." It was clear he was trying to hold back a grin that she wanted to wipe from his face.

Her mouth hung open as she looked at him. "I didn't know it was an option... no one ever said anything." Her eyes narrowed into slits. She wanted to throw something at him. The whole time she was here she could have had a kitchen? "You're going to pay for that." She took menacing steps towards him.

"Babe, be sensible. You have to admit it's funny." She chased him into his bedroom and they rolled onto the bed when she tackled him. They giggled as she lay on top of him. Once they're laughter died away, he pulled her down for a sweet kiss. His lips feathered kisses across her skin. "Did you want a shower?" He asked in between the drugging kisses he was giving her.

She shook her head. "Just want to fall asleep with you wrapped around me." She kissed him and rolled off of him and started removing her clothes. She stripped down to her panties and tank top. He smiled at her from across the bed where he was removing his clothes. The sexy boxer briefs he was wearing made her want to rethink going straight to sleep. When a yawn escaped, she knew tonight would not be a sex night. They pulled back the covers and crawled beneath them. His arms encircled her and she placed a kiss on his forearm. She wanted to stay in his arms all night.

Halfway through the night, she found herself dreaming. This time she knew he'd invaded her dreams and not the other way around. She stood in the middle of his throne room and tried to look defiant. It should have been expected. Katana and her minions had failed to get the book or her in Greece. Of course, he would try and get to her the only other way he knew how after that defeat.

He was always hard to read. The sly smile he sported didn't necessarily mean he was happy. He was just good at holding his cards close to the vest and giving nothing away. She puffed out her chest and stood taller, chin out, to try and prove her bravery.

Maybe, that was a bad idea. Killian stood and walked down the steps from his throne. If these dreams had taught her anything, it was to expect the unexpected. He took slow, deliberate steps meant to intimidate her.

"Where is the book?" His tone was menacing. He bared his teeth in a threat, reminding her what he was capable of, that he could butcher her. When he continued to approach she took a step back and cursed herself for a coward. She would have taken another, but found herself gripped tightly by her arms and held fast. Glancing back over her shoulder she found Katana glaring at her. "Going somewhere?"

She turned back around to face Killian, who now stood in front of her. "Tell me what I want to know." Nearly nose-to-nose with him she could see the flash of rage that he barely held in check.

Could he tear her limb from limb in a dream? Would her mortal body survive? It was possible she'd had all the bullying she could take from him, she couldn't tell for sure. But with a fearlessness and boldness that she didn't quite feel she stood up to him. "I will never tell you." Her eyes stared into his unwavering. A tremor started in her body moments ago, but it was okay. She would do her best to withstand whatever torture or punishment he intended to inflict to get what he wanted.

His nostrils flared in anger before he masked it. The sadistic smirk that crossed his face made her want to shrink away from him. It didn't take a rocket scientist to know he was about to hurt her. His hands gripped the sides of her head and his touch ignited a pain so vicious she cried out. If Katana hadn't been holding her she would have fallen to a limp heap on the floor. The last time he'd hurt her paled in comparison to the thousand flames that licked over her brain. She howled and screamed for relief.

"Tell me where the book is." He demanded and increased the torment. The agony was like a blowtorch frying her brain. It was possible he was going to kill her. Tears ran down her cheeks, mixing with the bloody nose that had started. She couldn't form the words to tell herself to wake up.

"Willow! Willow!" It took several seconds for her to realize it was Eli's voice calling her and not her punisher. She tried to focus, but her tears obstructed her vision. Her head was still on fire. For a moment, she felt like she was going to be sick.

"Willow." This time he spoke her name softly.

She finally managed to focus and her vision cleared. His face was horror-stricken. He cradled her in his arms. The inferno in her head was finally extinguished when she clearly saw his face. Tears seeped out of the corners of her eyes.

"I couldn't... I couldn't get you to wake up. You were screaming and crying... kicking and flailing about... I was..." He'd been scared. The words wouldn't form and move past his lips, but she knew. She could see it all over his face. Then she saw the bloody towel or whatever it was in his hand. Her trembling fingers reached up and touched her nose. When she pulled her fingers back to look, the smear of red stained her fingers.

It was all too much. Later, he would tell her she was in shock, but she started babbling, unable to shake the horror of how the torture had felt, but glad she'd stayed strong. "I was brave. I didn't tell him anything... I stayed strong." She shook her head and then began to keen and wail in a way she'd never done before. Her body shook with the effort to exorcise the event from her sub-conscious.

"Yes, you're very brave. The bravest person I know." He kissed her brow and crooned reassurances to her as he held her close. "You're safe... I'm here... You're safe." She wrapped herself around him tightly. It was a possibility she was hurting him, but he let her stay like that. Fear had her in its hold and wouldn't let go. She was frightened that if she let go of him she would find herself back in the nightmare, being tortured all over again. As long as she was in Eli's arms, Killian couldn't get her. Her grasp on him tightened every time she wandered to that dark place. It was a little after dawn when she finally wore herself out and fell asleep in his arms.

CHAPTER 12

Eli

HE SAT WITH his back against the headboard. She was cradled in his lap, her cheek pressed against his chest. When she'd finally fallen asleep he let out the breath he didn't realize he'd been holding. He cleaned her face and placed a kiss on her forehead, not knowing if she felt his presence as she slumbered. If he had to sit up the rest of the night, he decided he would sit vigil over her like an avenging angel ready to defeat any more bad dreams that came along.

Her hold on him had eased some, but he was afraid to let go of her, afraid she would wake up frightened if he wasn't nearby. A few times she whimpered, but he would stroke her hair or rub the backs of his fingers across her cheek and she would relax and burrow into him. After a while, he couldn't fight his sleepiness anymore and he dozed off.

The light from the window stung his eyes. He winced and pried his tired eyes open. When he looked down at her, he found her staring back. "You're awake?"

She nodded.

He looked around for a clock. "What time is it? How long have you been awake?"

"Not long."

They stared into each other eyes. Her fingers lightly stroked his chest. After a long silence he spoke. "Are you okay?" He didn't want her to feel like she had to talk about it if she didn't want to.

"You made it better... I'm really glad you were here." She kept her eyes pinned to his chest as she spoke.

"You didn't answer my question. I asked if you were okay?"

"I'm getting there." She gave him the barest smile.

It would do for now. She was trying to be courageous, but he wished she knew she didn't have to be, not with him.

He leaned forward and pressed his lips to her forehead and for a while they just held each other. Twenty minutes later, the mood in the room shifted from one of a comforting need to a carnal need. Last night she clung to him in fear, now all he could feel was her need for him. Her tongue darted out and licked his nipple. His cock became hard when her soft, warm lips sucked his nipple into her mouth and she gave him a love bite before releasing it with a pop. He pulled back and stared at her as his desire awakened. She did it again. The effect she had on him was drugging.

Sitting up, he kept his eyes locked on hers. His fingers slid down her stomach and underneath the waistband of her panties. His fingers were on a quest. When they reached their destination he could see her eyes get drowsy with lust. She was aching for him to touch her. The closer he got the harder her little cunt throbbed. He toyed with her. Using the wetness he found between her legs, he rubbed his wet finger in circles around her tight little bud. Never once actually touching the sensitive area he knew she wanted him to touch.

After he'd completed his eighth, slow circuit, her head was thrown back, her eyes closed and a small sheet of perspiration covered her. He knew she needed friction, the rough texture of his finger giving her enjoyment.

'ALL YOU HAVE TO DO IS ASK.'

She opened her eyes and peered at him. He dragged out another circle around her clit without giving her what she wanted. She bit her lip to keep from crying out. A tenth circle.

'PLEASE.'

'I WANT YOU TO SAY IT. I WANT TO HEAR THE MAGIC WORD FALL FROM YOUR PRETTY LIPS.' He rubbed around it again. She was so wet. When he was ready to shove his cock inside her he wouldn't be met with any resistance.

"Please." She said on a ragged breath.

'YOUR WISH IS MY COMMAND.' He gave her a wicked, lecherous grin before his finger rubbed her clit. She put her hand over his, trying to urge him on.

"UH UH." He admonished her. She hesitated and then her hand fell away. He slid one finger inside of her and stroked in and out slowly. Her pussy was so greedy for him it suctioned his finger in further each time. He added another finger and she moaned. The whole time he watched her face. Her lip curled in ecstasy. She began moving her hips. He curled his fingers so they hit her G-spot. That move had her moaning repeatedly. Soon, she was grinding her hips on his fingers. Any minute she would come. 'DOES THAT FEELS GOOD?' He knew the answer, but he wanted to hear her say it.

"So good."

He increased his pace and before he knew it she exploded on his fingers. He pumped them twice more into her before he pulled them out and sucked off her juices. She watched him beneath her lashes.

Once her legs stopped quivering he laid her on the bed and stripped off her panties. He removed his boxer briefs and nudged her thighs farther apart so he was on his knees between her thighs. As he reached for a condom in his bedside drawer she sat up and took his dick in her hands and stroked him. She put the tip within a centimeter of her lips and looked up at him. He held his breath, waiting to see what she would do. An involuntary movement had him pressing the tip against her lips. They held each other's gaze.

Clearly, now it was her turn to toy with him because she gave him an impish grin and let him stay pressed against her lips not doing anything. His balls ached. He could feel her breath on his dick and it had him throbbing. After another second she slowly ran her tongue around the tip before she swiped it like it was an ice cream cone. He bucked against her and let out the breath he'd been holding.

Damn! That felt good. That was just her tongue. What is her mouth going to feel like?

He willed her to go further, wrap her lips around him and suck. A broad grin broke out on his face when she gave his dick little licks with her tongue, teasing him much the way he'd teased her. 'WHAT'S THE MAGIC WORD?'

A chuckle sounded deep in his throat and then ceased when her tongue licked around the tip once more. He bit his lip and squeezed his eyes shut, enjoying the pleasurable sensations her mouth evoked. Then her mouth disappeared. His eyes flew open.

'YOU DON'T FIGHT FAIR.'

With deft fingers she stroked his cock and played with his balls.

'NEITHER DO YOU. WHAT'S IT GONNA BE?' She licked around the tip once more before she placed a kiss on the head and looked up at him innocently.

'PLEASE.'

'UH UH. I WANT YOU TO SAY IT. I WANT TO HEAR THE MAGIC WORD FALL FROM YOUR PRETTY LIPS.'

His head fell back as he laughed at hearing his earlier command given back to him verbatim. When he looked at her again, he could see the amusement written all over her face. She smiled up at him while her fingers applied the right amount of pressure. His dick was throbbing and pulsing with need. "Please."

The minute he said the word, she swallowed him. He groaned at how amazing her mouth felt. She stroked him and sucked him. The more he watched his dick slide in and out of her mouth the harder he became. One of his hands was buried in her hair. Her mouth felt so good he was reluctant to pull her off, but he wanted to be inside of her. Gently, he eased her off. She licked her lips and reached for him again.

"No, baby." His fingers caressed her cheek. "I don't want to cum like that. I want to cum buried inside of you." He tore open the wrapper and rolled the condom on hastily. When he pushed her back on the bed, she didn't resist. He positioned his cock at the entrance to her glistening pussy and kissed her before he slid deep inside. He heard her swift intake of breath as he filled her completely. It always felt like coming home to be connected to her in this way, their flesh one.

They were pressed chest to chest. Her thighs cradled him. He was in no hurry to move. Resting on his forearms, his eyes roamed her face. Her arms went around his neck and she lifted her head and kissed him. The hint of a smile peeked out before he nipped her lips and placed light kisses on and around her mouth, never taking his eyes from hers. Staring into her eyes heightened every sensation he was feeling. "You're so beautiful." He murmured into her lips.

Soon his tongue swiped inside her mouth and slowly he dominated and devoured her as he deepened the kiss.

After he finished his exploration of her mouth, he nuzzled her neck and delivered deep, slow strokes. Her tight, wet pussy was squeezing him. A grunt fell from his lips and he lightly bit her shoulder. He hooked her left leg over his forearm, opening her up even further. Their heavy breathing mixed with the slapping of sweaty skin upon sweaty skin. He could stay here all morning like this.

She was close. He made it a point to thrust hard and deep and rub the tip against her G-spot. In no time flat, she was thrashing her head back and forth beneath him as she came. Feeling her tighten around him sent him over the edge. He flooded the condom with his semen and buried his face in the crook of her neck as his body spasmed after his climax.

She still couldn't get enough of him. Although they'd both cum, her pussy continued to milk his cock dry. He jerked against her. The lingering tremors of his orgasm flowed through his body. He knew he needed to take off the condom, but the thought of pulling out of her right now was not possible. He kissed her sweat damp skin and inhaled the heady scent of her body. When she wrapped her hands around him, he held her tighter.

After a few more minutes, he pushed himself up on his hands and looked down in between their joined bodies. He didn't think that sight would ever get old. When he looked back up at her face, she gave him a lazy smile. He kissed her nose and her chin and then looked back down to watch as he slowly pulled his cock from her body.

Once he disposed of the condom in the bathroom, he came back into the room. Somehow they'd kicked the blankets and sheets to the edge of the mattress. Willow lay on her stomach, her arm folded beneath her head on the pillow, still naked. "I was right." He smirked and sat on the edge of the bed beside her. His fingers stroked between her shoulder blades.

"Hmm?"

"You do have the better ass." He leaned down and placed a kiss on each of her ass cheeks. When she giggled, he stroked his hand over her backside and smiled at her. "I'm gonna go see if I can find someone to spar with. Why don't you get some more sleep?"

"I think I will. You wore me out." She opened an eye and peeked at him. The way she looked right now he wanted to remember always: bee stung lips, mussed hair, damp, dewy skin, flushed cheeks and that love drunk look in her eyes. He was tempted to grab his cell phone and snap a shot. She turned on her side and reached for him. Without hesitation he bent over and she twined her arms around his neck. Even though they'd just enjoyed each other's bodies, the lingering kiss she gave him made him want to crawl back into bed with her.

She released him. "Go spar. I'm going to sleep." She shut her eyes again. He couldn't help himself. He leaned over and kissed her shoulder before he left.

***

"Easy man, easy." Max used his staff to repeatedly block Eli's moves that were intent on destruction. "We're just sparring."

He stopped. He was panting with the exertion of his movements. Despite making love to Willow before he left, he couldn't stop thinking about the person behind her night terrors.

There was all this aggression and anger inside of him that he didn't know what to do with. Last night, her broken sobs after the nightmare made him feel helpless and powerless. She was fighting an evil monster that none of them could yet defend against. The fact that he could get into her head like that and had been doing so for years infuriated him beyond anything he'd ever known. How could he fight her dreams?

"I don't know whose head you want to take off, but I'd like to keep mine on my shoulders." Max handed him a bottle of water.

"Thanks." After removing the cap he drank the water down in huge gulps. He wanted to ask Max a question, but he was almost afraid to hear the answer. He swiped the back of his hand over his mouth and watched Max tidy up the room. "When you were acting as Willow's dog... the dreams she had about Killian... did they often become violent?" He looked down to avoid Max's gaze.

Silence ensued for so long, for a moment he wondered if Max chose not to answer the question. When he looked back up, Max was eyeing him wearily. It was the most serious he'd seen him look. "She had a nightmare last night?" They held each other's gaze. Eli nodded.

"There were night's she'd wake up screaming, thrashing around in the sheets. I believed it was mostly out of fear. Nothing ever indicated he got physical with her..." He looked at the floor for a second before looking back at him. "That first night on the road when she had the bad dream was the first time it appeared he was hurting her."

Involuntarily, Eli's hands balled into fists. He wanted to hit something until this anger disappeared from his body.

In a burst of anger, he gave way to the fury he felt and slammed the staff in his hand against the ground repeatedly as he yelled out his frustration. Soon there was nothing left of the piece of wood that had withstood many fights. It was splintered into broken bits that were scattered across the floor. What was left in his hand was a fractured piece of the weapon. A small jagged piece protruded from his palm and blood welled up from the puncture wound. He stood staring at it for long seconds before Max came over.

"Let me get the first aid kit."

Eli pulled out the jagged piece of wood. "It's fine. I can just heal it." He placed his other hand over the wound. "Sana." A white light glowed from underneath his palm over the puncture wound. When he removed his hand, he was healed.

Max stared at his hand impressed. "That will never get old."

He was happy for the distraction of Max's good-natured vibe. It was exactly what he needed. He smiled at him and was about to ask if he wanted to do some boxing when Archie shuffled in. "The Council wants to see you and the Protectors in one hour." He delivered the curt message and walked out.

Any other day he would have ribbed Archie for not greeting them or teased the old man, but today he was in no mood to be jovial. He was sure The Council wanted a report on what happened in Greece. Now that they knew the book was in Egypt he needed to start making plans. The sooner they got there and found the book the sooner they could end Killian.

He was about to clean up the mess he made when Phaedra walked in. "We need to talk."

"Okay." She seemed more serious than usual. "What's up?"

She glanced over in Max's direction without saying another word. It was clear whatever she had to say were for his ears only. Max seemed to take the hint. He grabbed his towel and left.

"They know."

"What?"

"Someone talked."

"Can you stop being cryptic and assuming I know what your coded messages are about. If you were going to be like that, you could have let Max stay. What are you talking about?" He continued to pick up the broken pieces of the staff.

"Someone from Greece called and spoke to The Council about you and Willow."

He stopped what he was doing and looked at her.

"They know you're involved with her."

For a while he said nothing, then he resumed picking up the bits of wood.

"Aren't you going to say anything? Aren't you worried?"

He tried not to be angry with her, she was only the messenger, but he couldn't help his agitated tone. "What? What do you want me to say? You want me to tell you that I'm going to stop being with her to appease The Council and my father? Well I'm not. I love her and she loves me."

"You know it's not that simple, Elias. This goes beyond The Council."

His jaw ticked. "I guess I'll just have to face the consequences." He glared at her for a second before he turned his back on her and continued cleaning up.

"You're being stubborn... Don't do this." For the first time since he'd known her, he heard real fear in her voice. He knew he should be concerned too, but he wouldn't let his father, The Council or the law dictate to him. When he continued to do what he was doing without acknowledging her last statement, he heard her walk away. She slammed the door open with such force on her way out, it rattled on its hinges. He appreciated that his friend was worried about what price he'd have to pay for choosing love above duty, but he wouldn't change his mind.

His thoughts went back to that morning, when he'd woken to find her in his arms, staring up at him. If it hadn't been for the horrible nightmare, it had been the perfect way to wake up: looking at her beautiful face. He'd almost lost her once. He wouldn't chance it again.

CHAPTER 13

Willow

AFTER HE LEFT, she fell asleep without the fear of Killian invading her dreams. Considering he'd escalated the level of pain and horror he subjected her to, she was thankful to wake up in Eli's arms after being terrorized.

When she'd woken, Eli hadn't returned so she took a shower. As much as she wanted to keep thinking about how good Eli made her feel sexually and otherwise, Killian kept occupying her thoughts.

That bastard meant to terrorize her. He'd won again last night. At least he hadn't been around to see the aftermath of his torture. She knew one thing: she wasn't going to let Killian break her. The long shower helped her clear her head.

When she emerged from the bathroom someone was knocking on the door.

Did he forget his key? Last time I was here I didn't need a key to get into my room. Why is he knocking?

She opened the door. "Is there a reason you're..." The rest of what she was about to say died on her tongue when she saw Phaedra standing on the other side of the door. "Hey... um, Eli's not here. He stepped out for a minute."

"I know. I'm here to see you." Phaedra stepped inside without a smile and without invitation.

"Okay." Willow shut the door behind her. This felt ominous. She was only wearing a bathrobe and after last night she still felt vulnerable. At least if she was fully clothed she'd feel like she had a shield or some sort of protection against whatever Phaedra was going to say to her. She wrapped his robe tighter around her body. "What is it?"

"I think you should break things off with Eli." Her stare was unapologetic.

She wasn't sure what she'd been expecting to hear come out of Phaedra's mouth, but it wasn't that. Her mouth hung open in shock and surprise. Phaedra was with Max, so it couldn't be jealousy that had her in Eli's place telling her to break up with him. "Why would I do that?" She turned away from her, trying to mask her hurt. Even though they weren't friendly like she was with the other Protectors, she at least thought Phaedra liked her and that they were becoming friends.

"You're new to this world. There are things you don't yet understand." Sometimes she wondered if the woman was a robot. Phaedra spoke in such an emotionless, matter of fact, no-nonsense tone it annoyed her, given what the woman was asking her to do.

"Does this have something to do with the anti-hybrid stuff that Eli was talking about?" A horrifying thought struck her. "Are you one of them?" She hissed at Phaedra and leaned away from her in alarm. Revulsion settled like a stone in her stomach.

"No." Phaedra rolled her eyes so hard, for a minute she was afraid they would roll right out of her head.

"Why don't you approve of us being together?" She was so confused.

Phaedra looked torn and exasperated. "This has nothing to do with me... I can't say more than that... Things are about to get really bad for him. If you care about him, you'll do this."

The anger she felt was going to erupt any minute and she'd rather not have to apologize later. She crossed over to the door and ripped it open. Her body was trembling she was so furious. "I think you should leave." Her voice shook a little on the end. The tight grip she had on the doorknob was sure to leave an imprint in her palm if she didn't break off the knob first.

"Just think about what I said." Those were Phaedra's parting words. Willow slammed the door behind her.

***

When Eli arrived twenty minutes later she was fully dressed in a plaid shirt and jeans. The anxiety she felt as she waited for him seemed to increase with every minute. The door opened and she jumped up from her seat on the sofa. "Hey." She wondered if Phaedra had already talked to him. What had she said to him and how had he responded. She looked at his face trying to gauge what had transpired since he'd left. His face gave away nothing.

"We have to appear in front of The Council in fifteen minutes. I need to get cleaned up." He went to step past her.

"Wait. That's all? Do you know what it's about?" She knew after Phaedra's visit there was going to be more to this meeting with The Council than he was letting on. "Tell me what's going on." He kept his back to her for several seconds before he finally turned around.

"Promise me whatever happens you'll be as brave as you were last night." That seemed to be the only explanation he was going to give her.

She came over and put her arms around his waist. Her eyes pleaded with him. "You're scaring me. What's going on?"

He rubbed her cheek. "Just trust me okay. I love you." He kissed her and gently pulled her arms from around him and went to take a quick shower.

If she'd had more time she could have sought out Morgana, Zoriana or even Mathilda to find out what was going on, but something told her she wasn't sure they would be so forthcoming with answers either.

After he showered they walked to The Council's Chamber. She felt like a dead man walking. Eli didn't say a word on the way there. He kept his focus straight ahead. She wondered what he was thinking about.

Before they entered the room, he took her hand in his and gave her a sad smile. She wanted to pull him away from the door and demand he tell her what was going to happen in that room, but she knew it was useless. He was used to being the Protector and that's what he was doing now, trying to protect her. Why did she feel like he was the one that needed protecting?

When they stepped through the door, hands clasped, all eyes were on them. She didn't miss Silas' hard look of disapproval the minute he saw their hands linked. All the other Protectors stood in a row in front of Elders of The Council. When they joined them and she glanced down the row, they all looked uneasy. Max was the only one that smiled in her direction and offered a slight wave. The corner of her mouth tried to tilt into a smile, but it was hard since she knew she wasn't going to like how this turned out.

Phaedra stood with her hands clasped behind her back; legs shoulder width apart like she was waiting for a military inspection. Her face was hard and unreadable. The rest were just trying to avoid her looks. They knew something was up and no one had tried to warn her. An edgy feeling settled over her and she looked down at Eli's and her conjoined hands. He squeezed her hand and she looked up into his eyes. The flash of a smile he gave her before he turned back to face The Council might have put her at ease if she wasn't already sure that this was not going to go well.

The members of The Council took their seats now ready to call their meeting to order.

"First things first, did you recover The Book of Prophecy?" Silas had yet to take his eyes off his son.

"No, the book is no longer in Greece and it's possible it hasn't been in some time."

"So where is it?"

She continued to grow antsy. Everyone was talking about the book, while the elephant in the room continued to grow at an alarming rate.

"We believe it's in Egypt..."

"You believe? You don't know for sure?" Silas condescension grated on her nerves.

"We won't know until we go there. Willow..." His father interrupted him again. When he said her name with an edge in his voice she stood a little straighter.

"The Council was made aware of the change in your relationship with Ms. Stevens. Would you like to confirm or deny this?"

Ms. Stevens? Since when did things become so formal she couldn't but wonder sarcastically?

Eli didn't hesitate or stutter, he answered clearly. "I love her and I have it on pretty good authority that she loves me." His chest seemed to puff out a little bit when he said the words.

She couldn't help herself. Even though he couldn't see her, a broad grin broke out on her face at his declaration.

Put that in your pipe and smoke it, Silas.

She wanted to give the man the middle finger, but he was still Eli's father after all so she would show him respect. How did Josephine, Eli's mother put up with his pompous ass?

"You're aware of the Protector's Commandment that you swore an oath to that states: A Protector shall not enter a relationship or fall in love with the Oracle?"

"I am."

Willow's jaw dropped open. It's a commandment? Wildly she scanned the room. She felt dizzy.

"You're aware of the law enacted by the Congress of Supernatural Beings this commandment was derived from that states: No supernatural shall enter a relationship or fall in love with the Oracle?"

"Yes."

Her head was swimming and she felt sick to her stomach. There was a law that punished someone who wanted to be with her? Love her? "This is bullshit!" She exploded.

'DON'T.' He came through in her head, trying to warn her away from whatever she was about to do.

She ignored him and approached The Council. " Was no one ever going to tell me what had been decided about my life? What gives you the right? A law? A law that I don't have any say in? That's set in place to keep me from loving and being with who I want?" She didn't care that her voice was loud or that she might have been disrespectful. She wanted answers. Why had this law been put in place and why were they enforcing something so archaic?

One of the Elders spoke up, trying to reason with her. "It was set in place for a reason. All the supernaturals agreed. It was done for your own good..."

"For my own good?" Her voice lashed out like a whip.

Before she could launch into a further attack on The Council, Eli grabbed her hand. She looked at him, a little hurt, but feeling responsible for the mess they now found themselves in. "Why didn't you tell me?"

"Maybe for the same way you're acting now." His face twitched into a smirk.

Was this what Phaedra had been trying to warn her about? Her eyes skittered over to the hard woman, but she wasn't looking at them.

Why didn't I listen?

Was he really making jokes right now? "This is serious, Eli. I can't let you do this. I won't. Just take it all back. Tell them you're sorry. Say whatever you need to say to stay out of trouble." She turned towards The Council again ready to tell them they were not together. "He's lying..."

He yanked her into his chest and dropped his voice so only she could hear him. "That would be telling a lie. I won't do it. I know I may have said that I love you for the first time in that hotel room, but Willow I loved you long before that. I fell in love with you probably after the first year of watching you, but I lied to myself and I tried to bury it away. I won't live like that again." He swallowed as he stared into her eyes. "Whatever the consequences are, I'll take them." He turned back to The Council. "I have broken the Protector's Commandment and I have broken the law. I will answer for my crimes."

She squeezed her eyes shut for a moment, in frustration over his stubbornness and also out of fear. He still held her hand. She moved closer and wrapped her other arm around his.

"So be it." His father's voice sounded weary and regretful. It was clear he took no great pleasure in what he was about to say. "You are hereby removed from your position as head of The Protectors. Phaedra will now take over. As the final consequence for your action you will no longer have access to the ancestors. You will be stripped..." Although she couldn't see his face fully, she noticed the last statement had a visceral effect on him.

She heard the other Protectors gasp in shock.

What does that mean? I don't understand.

"What does that mean? Tell me what that means." She begged him, but he was still trying to recover from the shock. Two witches materialized from out of the shadows and were about to seize him.

"Give me a minute." He didn't ask. He made the demand calmly and the witches who'd come to take him away halted.

"What does all of this mean? Why didn't you tell me about this stupid law?" Her lip trembled as she tried not to cry. She was trying to be brave like he asked her to. "I would have never pushed you..."

"You didn't push me into anything." He cleared his throat. "Remember I told you magic comes at a cost?" She nodded because her throat was clogged with unshed tears.

"Well sometimes love comes at a cost too." Tears stood in his eyes. "I will gladly pay the price." He stepped towards her and cupped her face in his hands. His eyes held hers and his thumbs rubbed her cheeks. She couldn't stop the flood of tears. "You're worth it." He whispered into her lips before he pressed his lips against hers in a searing kiss that let everyone know how he felt about her.

When they pulled him away after a few seconds, she tried to grab onto him and Mathilda and Zoriana rushed to comfort her and keep her from running after him.

"Mathilda what's happening?" She tried not to be hysterical as Eli was taken from the room. She wanted to yell, stamp her feet, punch someone or something, run after him and make them bring him back.

Zoriana spoke first. "He's no longer a Protector." Her head jerked back like she'd been punched. He'd worked so hard his whole life for that designation. "But... I just thought he wouldn't be the leader anymore." She said weakly. "But where are they taking him. Silas said stripping." She looked around at their faces.

"Stripping is a form of punishment for witches found practicing black magic and for breaking certain supernatural laws." Morgana's voice was hollow when she spoke.

"He's going to be stripped of his hereditary magic." A tear fell down Mathilda's cheek.

"What?" She said barely above a whisper. She was breathless now.

Max came over and hugged her. "Everything's going to be okay." She let herself be held by Max. Normally, his proximity would have calmed her, but right now her heart and her head were in turmoil. Morgana stroked her hair and Mathilda and Zoriana were both close by rubbing her back.

She didn't have to look at Phaedra to know the woman blamed her. She'd come to her today and asked her to call things off. Why hadn't she made her understand? This was all because of her. She couldn't let him do this. Not for her. Before she allowed despair to swallow her whole, she thought about Cora. She was the real head of The Council. She would go to her and beg her to put a stop to this. She probably had no idea what was happening.

She broke out of their grasp and ran from the room.

"Willow." Zoriana tried to stop her. She didn't slow down. For a minute she worried someone would chase her down and try to stop her from going where she was headed, but no one followed her. Up the staircase she ran. The whole time her head full of thoughts.

Cora is the Chief Elder. They have to listen to her. She can reverse this. She can make them let Eli keep his magic.

When she burst through the door a nurse was taking the woman's blood pressure. If the situation weren't so dire she would have been astonished to find someone in the woman's bedchamber, but right now she was too upset. The nurse seemed ready to try and stop her from reaching Cora, but the old woman waved her away and she dropped back to the shadows.

"Cora, please do something. You have to do something. They're going to take away his magic." She sobbed into the old woman's lap.

Cora patted her shoulder. "There, there child. It will be alright. He still has magic. It's just not as powerful as it was."

Slowly, Willow sat up. "What?" She gave the crone an incredulous look.

"I said he still has magic. It will be okay."

How could... How could Cora know who or what she was talking about, unless... "You did this." The accusation nearly choked her when she said it. Why did she think this woman cared? Because she shared some things about her mother and gave her some letters? She felt like the biggest fool.

"It's the law. I'm afraid it's out of my hands." The woman didn't look the least bit apologetic over Eli's fate.

She swiped the angry tears away and left the room with Cora calling her to come back.

Despite getting lost twice because her tears kept blinding her and she refused to take anyone's help, she finally found her way back to Eli's and collapsed on the sofa. She gave way to her emotions and wept until she passed out.

CHAPTER 14

Eli

HE SHOULD PROBABLY care about who called The Council. Who was so bothered by their relationship that they had to alert them? Not that they wouldn't have found out eventually. He was never trying to keep it hidden.

Repeatedly, he'd lied to himself that the consequences wouldn't be that bad. That he would receive a slap on the wrist. His way of thinking hadn't just been because his father sat on The Council. He just didn't think it would matter so much, but the law was the law, especially when it was a law controlled by the Congress of Supernatural Beings. It could be worse. The Council could have given him over to Congress and let them mete out punishment. Instead they chose to deal with it internally. He knew they would be satisfied with his pound of flesh.

What could be worse than losing his tie to his ancestors, losing his hereditary magic would feel like losing a piece of himself, but it couldn't be worse than having to let Willow go. He might as well cut out his heart.

The two witches that flanked him led him to the stripping chamber. They hadn't used the room in years, since the Black Magic Rebellion had been put down.

He didn't want Willow to blame herself for this. It was his decision.

As they walked him through the square, he could see the curious stares and hear the whispers of gossip people exchanged. He held his head high. Stripping scared him, but he would face it. The witches led him into the room and left. He'd never been in this chamber. No magic could be performed in this room. He clenched his fists and looked around the room as he paced nervously.

The room resembled a surgical viewing room at a hospital except it was circular and this viewing room gave you a three hundred and sixty degree view. The windows that encircled the top of the room for viewing were shatter proof. The air in the room tasted old and stale from disuse. There was another scent that lingered in the air that he couldn't decipher. It was the energy within the four walls that disquieted his spirit, almost as if he could feel the acute loss that others had suffered in the room.

Soon The Council would file in and fill the space in the viewing chamber so they could perform the stripping.

In an area of the room he saw a metal table with hand and ankle straps. He fingered one of the ankle straps.

"That's there for those that won't accept the stripping and try to fight." The old woman's voice was strong and belied her years. He looked up into the viewing room. Cora hadn't been there a moment ago. "I'm sorry my sweet boy. If I could save you from this I would."

Somehow he knew that Willow had begged her for mercy. "She came to see you?"

She nodded.

It made him smile to think of her fighting for him.

Moments later, the other Elders filed in and took their places.

"Are we ready to begin?"

Everyone nodded in answer.

"This will hurt a little. Don't try and fight it. You'll only make it worse."

He found his father and when he saw his face he was shocked to find tears in his father's eyes. His father never looked away as they began the chant that would remove his connection to his ancestors and strip him of his hereditary magic. "Maiorum, audierit a senioribus. Est autem repleti sunt ut indignus te et potestatem spirituum. Auferte hereditate sua tacere et audire non possunt vocibus et industria.

The minute the first incantation concluded and they started the chant again, he understood why they called it stripping... and why it was painful.

The only thing he could find to compare it to was having part of his soul ripped from his body. Though that had never happened before, he was certain this was exactly how it would feel. The bond that tethered him like so many others from the Walker coven was being stripped away piece by piece and soon nothing would remain. He would no longer have the link. Over the years, he and his father had had their differences, but he knew by the look on his father's face no matter how much they may have fought or he disagreed with his choices, he knew how much his father loathed the chore of stripping him. He was here doing his duty as an Elder, but he took no joy or pleasure in it.

He ground his teeth against the torment, but despite his attempts not to give into the pain he screamed.

CHAPTER 15

Willow

SOMEONE WAS POUNDING on the door. When she opened her eyes and looked around she realized it was the next morning.

What time is it? How long did I sleep?

She was still in her clothes from yesterday and had slept on the couch. The knocking came again. If she slept on the sofa last night, that meant that Eli hadn't come home. There was someone at the door, but she ran to the bedroom first just to be sure he wasn't there.

The bed was made up. She looked into the bathroom. No Eli. She dragged herself to the door worried about why he wouldn't have come home. The knocking at this point had grown incessant. She threw open the door, ready to bitch at whoever was on the other side of it. She was in a foul mood and worried that Eli hadn't come home because he didn't want to face her.

Zoriana and Morgana walked past her into the living room the minute she opened the door. She bit her tongue and huffed.

What do they want, the Judases?

She was salty with them over not informing her about this heinous law and their lack of action yesterday in trying to stop the stripping thing from happening to Eli. The rational side of her brain understood they couldn't go up against the Elders or this Congress of Supernaturals that was mentioned, but it didn't keep her from being pissed. Eli was one of their own. He was their leader. "What do you want?"

All she wanted to do is to go find him and try and make sure he wasn't angry or didn't resent her and want to break up with her. She remembered everything he said before they took him away, but what if he was feeling differently afterwards?

"We came here to cheer you up and to let you know that Phaedra wants to head to Egypt the day after tomorrow."

I'll bet she does. She couldn't wait to be the one running things.

She folded her arms across her chest. "I'm not going anywhere without Eli." She glared hard at Morgana then Zoriana to make sure they got the message.

"Listen, we know you're upset..."

Before she could launch into her rant, the door was kicked open. Phaedra and Ulrik held Eli between them, his arms slung over their shoulders. He was unconscious. She rushed forward to help them.

"Let us get him to his bed. Then he is all yours." Ulrik offered.

She took a step back, but remained on their heels. When they laid him back against the pillows she could see his face looked haggard and ashen.

"Ladies, I'm sorry to hear about what has happened to our friend here. He is an honorable man." Ulrik gave her a sympathetic look before he turned to Phaedra. "We'll talk later about plans for Egypt."

Willow waited until he left. She knew that Morgana and Zoriana lingered in the living room so she pushed the door closed so they wouldn't be overheard. "What plans for Egypt? I'll tell you like I told the two of them. I don't go unless he goes..." She sneered at Phaedra. "You just couldn't wait to call the shots. You're ready to take off..."

"Don't you dare." It was the first time, besides the battlefield, that she'd witnessed Phaedra's emotions. She was seething with rage, although she still managed to hold it in check. The woman was such a closed book she never knew where she stood with her or what she was feeling.

"Elias is my best friend. I warned him, I begged him to let you go. I came to you to get you to let him go. Don't tell me how I feel." Her nostrils flared as she glowered at Willow. "I don't care about being head of The Protectors. It never interested me to be in charge." Phaedra advanced on her until her back hit the wall. "The only reason I'm making plans to head to Egypt is because it's where the book is located, so says you. I know it's what he would want if he was still in charge because he cares about you and he would want to move as quickly as possible if it meant keeping you safe."

Willow wished she could eat her words. It was too soon to try and apologize. She'd let her own anger keep her from seeing the pain that everyone else was in.

"It goes without saying that I wouldn't leave on the mission without Elias. Protector or no Protector, he's like my brother and I would never betray him. He knows that and now that I've educated you on the matter I'm going to leave. You can tell him I will check on him later and discuss the mission with him then." She didn't wait for Willow to say she was sorry or anything else, she left the bedroom. The door in the living room shook with the force of her slam when she left Eli's apartment.

She felt like an ass for accusing Phaedra of wanting Eli's position. She'd just been so angry over everything she hadn't been thinking clearly. The woman had laid her life on the line for her more than once and that was how she repaid her. She had to make it up to her somehow. Her eyes looked down at Eli once more before she turned out the light and shut the door to the bedroom.

Zoriana and Morgana were great at pretending they hadn't heard any of what happened between her and Phaedra.

"I'm sorry I was rude to the two of you earlier. It wasn't fair. You've only ever tried to look out for me and I acted like a bitch. Now I have to find some way to make it up to Phaedra." She sighed and looked at them. "Forgive me?"

They both came over and hugged her.

"Of course we do. Yesterday was hard on all of us." Morgana was being very understanding.

It was her first smile since everything had happened. "I really appreciate you guys coming by. Now that Eli is here, I think I'm going to shower, change and make some food in case he's hungry when he wakes up."

"No problem. Call us if you need anything." Morgana offered before she headed to the door.

Zoriana lingered for a moment. "I know I haven't exactly been available..." She looked slightly embarrassed, and Willow's heart went out to her. "I haven't been handling this rift between Mathilda and I very well, but if you or Eli need anything please don't hesitate to reach out. I mean that. Eli's my nephew and you're..." For a minute she seemed uncertain about whether she should say the next line. "You've become family too, okay?" She squeezed her hand and then left before Willow could respond.

Zoriana's comment left her dumbstruck. It touched her deeply that the woman considered her family. It had been so long since she had one. The Protectors may not be blood related to her, but they were certainly starting to feel like the closest thing to family she had in a long time.

She went back into the bedroom and tried not to stand their watching Eli like a stalker. When would he wake up? How would he feel when he woke up? Would he still want to be with her? All these questions swirled around her head. She was about to head into the bathroom when someone else knocked on the door.

Who could this be?

She looked around on the way to the door wondering if Zoriana or Morgana had forgotten anything or if this time it was Max or Mathilda wanting to cheer her up. When she opened the door she was surprised to find Josephine there. The woman had been crying. Terror filled her at the thought of his mother hating her and wanting her gone, out of his life. "Mrs. Walker..." Words failed her. She waited for the stinging slap to mark her cheek.

Josephine stepped into the room and hugged Willow. Her grip was almost crushing. The woman's grief clung to her like a second skin.

"They said my boy was here." She squeezed Willow a little more tightly.

"Yes, Phaedra and Ulrik just brought him back. He's still sleeping. Would you like to see him?"

Josephine nodded and allowed herself to be led to the bedroom. She turned on the light and his mother immediately settled next to him on the bed. She took his hand in hers and with her other hand she brushed his hair from his forehead. Willow felt like she was intruding on something that should be private so she backed out of the room and pulled the door behind her to give mother and son their privacy.

She decided to busy herself with cooking. Even though they'd only returned a couple nights ago, neither of them had been in the kitchen and they'd been gone for a while so she was quite surprised to open the refrigerator and cabinets to find them fully stocked. Her mind went back to Zoriana and Morgana, they'd probably done it while she was being chastised by Phaedra. She pulled items from the refrigerator for a salad. Something healthy would probably do him good. She wasn't sure what stripping did to him, but if his unconscious state and pallid appearance were any indication he would probably be famished when he woke up. As a main dish she decided to make a baked lemon chicken dish when she found fresh lemons in the fruit bowl.

The chicken had just been put into the oven to bake and she was chopping up ingredients for the salad when his mother exited the bedroom. She sniffled as she walked into the kitchen. "He's still asleep." She used a handkerchief to dab at her red-rimmed eyes. Her glasses set on top of her head instead of perched on the tip of her nose like she'd seen them the night of the dinner party.

She waited for his mother to yell at her. Tell her this was all her fault. She would take whatever abuse the woman wanted to throw at her. It was her fault. She knew that.

Quietly, she put down the knife she'd been using and waited. She couldn't bring herself to meet her eyes.

"Look at me." His mother's voice was authoritative and didn't seem to tolerate people not listening when she made a demand.

She raised her eyes to peer at the woman, expecting to see hate and disdain, but instead she saw love, kindness and compassion.

"I know you're hurting too... and you probably blame yourself. I hope you don't." She took a deep breath before continuing. "My son has always been strong-willed and he makes up his own mind about things... He made up his mind to love you despite the consequences. So, do me a favor and don't get crazy thoughts in that pretty little head of yours. When he wakes up he's going to feel out of sorts, but he will not regret the decision he made. He'll live with his choices. I need you to live with yours and don't second guess, play games of what if, shoulda, coulda, woulda or any of that nonsense... Be the woman he sacrificed..." Tears trickled down her face once more. She wiped at them with the handkerchief. "Be the woman he sacrificed part of himself for and love him like I know he loves you. That's all I ask."

Willow found herself crying at his mother's words. "I promise." The woman opened her arms to her once again and Willow went willingly. Her mother wasn't here to comfort her, but she felt like her mother's words would have mirrored Josephine's.

After she left, Willow finished preparing the meal and went to take a shower. When she walked out of the bathroom wearing one of his t-shirts and some panties she was surprised to find him sitting up on the edge of the bed.

CHAPTER 16

Eli

HIS BRAIN WAS foggy and achy and his psyche felt
fried. It took a moment for everything to come flooding
back to him: the meeting with The Elders, Willow weeping,
the agony of the stripping.

That's why I feel like I've been split in half.

How long had he been asleep? The sun was no longer
out so either it was the same night or the next day. He was
about to go in search of Willow if his legs supported him
when she emerged from the bathroom.

For a while they just stared at one another.

"How do you feel?" She hung back in the doorway like
she was too afraid or nervous to come further into the
bedroom. Her eyes met his for a brief second and then
skittered away.

"I feel like I don't want my girlfriend to walk on eggshells around me." He glanced at her and this time she held his gaze. "Come here."

She hesitated for only a second and then she came to him. He reached out his hand to her and she took it. He wasn't sure what he was feeling yet and knew he would need time to really process not having hereditary magic anymore and not being a Protector, but one thing he was sure about was choosing to love her.

"I'm sorry." Fell from her lips the minute she sat on his lap. He could see tears spiked her lashes.

"Shhh." He shook his head at her. "Don't ever be sorry for loving me. I'm not sorry I love you..." He kept staring into her eyes. "It might have hurt like hell, but I would do it again in a heartbeat to stay with you."

She cupped his face in her hands and gave him a soft, sweet, soulful kiss that she poured her everything into. He could feel it and it reminded him of the first time she kissed him and confessed her love for him. His arms wrapped around her and he just held her.

After several minutes she pulled back to look at him. "Do you want to take a shower? I cooked. I figured you'd be hungry."

"Yeah. Go on and I'll be out there in a minute."

She obediently got up from his lap and closed the door behind her, leaving him alone. He tried not to let his mind dwell on the missing piece of him he could feel. It was like being a new amputee that just lost an arm or a leg. Phantom limb pain, that's what they called it. Maybe if he didn't think about it, it would go away.

Shakily, he stood. It took him a moment to right himself and regain his balance. He was still just a little weak from the stripping. Once he was sure he wouldn't topple over he went into the bathroom. When he stared into the mirror he didn't look different, but he was. He could feel it.

He turned on the shower and removed his clothes. Beneath the warm spray of the water he hung his head and let it wash him clean; wash his feelings down the drain. If only it were that easy.

The rage was building up inside of him. He could feel it. If he let it eat him from the inside out, he would be no good to her.

He beat his fist against the tile and screamed out his hurt, frustration and anger, exorcised the foul demons from his body. She still needed him and he wanted to be whole for her. Not dead on the inside. He would learn to live with this. This was the new him.

***

If she heard him scream in the shower that night she never said anything about it. He was grateful to her for not hovering or asking every five minutes if he was okay. After that night, they didn't speak about it again.

That same night, even though he was no longer a Protector, he sat with them and made plans for getting to Egypt to retrieve The Book of Prophecy. Surprisingly, Ulrik had been instrumental in getting the help of a local coven there.

Eli appreciated his team. None of them had treated him with kid gloves or pity. They treated him the same as they always had. Two days later they found themselves on this flight to Egypt.

He looked over at Willow. She'd read quite a bit on the flight, especially about her Oracle abilities. They'd even discussed some of it. Another book on Oracles sat opened in her lap. He took her hand in his and kissed the back of it.

"What was that for?" She grinned at him.

"No reason, just because."

Her eyes sparkled and she went back to reading. When he peaked over the armrest to get a better look, he realized she was actually looking at one of her mother's letters again. He would just never understand why she hid them.

She knew she'd been caught. "I'm sorry." She looked at him sheepishly and pulled the letter out and laid it on top of the now closed book. The light filtered in from the window and made some of Hyacinth's handwriting more legible on the yellowing paper.

"You have nothing to apologize for... I guess I just don't understand why you hide it." He searched her face looking for answers, wondering if she would tell him. She looked at her lap, her fingers toying with the frayed edge.

Her eyes stayed on her lap when she spoke. "When I read these letters, I imagine we're having a conversation... It makes me feel like I have some small piece of her walking around with me..." She gave a nervous chuckle and started to fold the letter. "That sounds stupid."

"Baby," he took her hand in his once more. "I don't think there's anything silly, stupid or crazy about that. It's your mom. I remember what you told me about feeling like you were losing her, like she was starting to slip away. Getting these letters gives her back to you... I get it."

She leaned into him. "Thank you for being so understanding."

"Anything for you."

Fifteen minutes later, they touched down in Cairo. The travel time had been long and he was anxious to sleep in a bed, so they could refresh and be ready to start their mission. They all packed light and had no checked baggage so they made it through customs without any issues. When they exited the customs area Ulrik walked over to two people with outstretched arms. They spoke to each other in a language that Eli hadn't heard before.

When the rest of the group caught up to them, Ulrik made introductions. "Please allow me to introduce my friends Anippe and Gamal. They are members of the Badawi coven." The pair looked like they were possibly brother and sister. Their skin tone was a beautiful russet brown. Both had black hair. Gamal's was cut into a style worn by many men in the area. Anippe's hair was straight and fell past her shoulders. They both wore jeans. He was in a t-shirt with the logo for Egypt's football team, the Pharoah's on the center and she was in a white, short-sleeved button up shirt. The thing he found most striking about them was that they looked like they could be related to Willow.

"What language were you speaking? It didn't sound familiar to me." Eli asked looking back and forth between the two and Ulrik.

"I spent a specific amount of time here. It was one of the first places I came to during my exile and Anippe was kind enough to teach me the Nubian language, Nobiin, their family spoke with each other during my stay." It didn't go unnoticed that Anippe's face flushed at his comments. It was clear there was more between the two than just friendship.

"They are both well versed in languages: Arabic, English and French." He made the declaration like a proud father.

"You are too kind, Uli. This coming from a man, who knows fifteen languages." Anippe heaped praise on the Dane.

Eli raised an eyebrow at the nickname she called him.

This time he blushed. "When you've lived as long as I have you have nothing but time on your hands."

Gamal looked uncomfortable when he finally spoke. "I apologize that are coven will not be offering you hospitality..." He looked down at the ground for a minute before giving Ulrik an apologetic look. The news upset Ulrik, and he and Gamal conversed rapidly in the Nobiin tongue. Ulrik ran his hand through his hair in frustration before he addressed the group.

"While we were on our way here their coven was made aware of Willow's hybrid status and... the fact that the two of you are together. Since it is against the law it would make some of the members uncomfortable if we stayed there... They would feel like they are condoning the relationship."

That damn law.

It had been put in place because everyone was scared the Oracle would show favoritism or loyalty to the particular faction her lover belonged to, but it was so antiquated in its thinking. In his opinion, it was enacted because Oracles were women and thought incapable of making decisions that weren't ruled by their hearts. It was bullshit. If the Oracle was a man, there's no way the law would have been passed.

At hearing people disapproved of their relationship, he felt Willow's body tense because he was holding her hand. He squeezed her hand to reassure her. He'd already paid the price. No one was going to make them feel like their love was wrong. They could all go to hell as far as he was concerned.

Ulrik continued. "The coven is divided because some have the belief that supernaturals should not mix..." He pinched the bridge of his nose and spoke under his breath, "Fanden."

When Eli saw Anippe's reaction to Ulrik's distress something clicked. All of Ulrik's venom over the anti-hybrid supernatural groups and hateful views of the inter-mixing of supernaturals wasn't merely just because that way of thinking was archaic, small-minded and stupid, but that he'd been on the receiving end of it himself, clearly with Anippe. She looked like she wanted to comfort him, but stayed next to Gamal. Her eyes constantly darted to him and her hands were restless at her sides.

After he composed himself, Ulrik finished telling them the situation. "...To keep the peace, their father, has decided that we cannot stay at the coven house, but he will take care of our accommodations. He has tasked Gamal and Anippe to help us, but that is the only support we'll have from his coven while we are here." Eli's ears burned with his anger. Willow bristled beside him. Gamal looked shame-faced. It wasn't their fault some of the members of their coven were idiots.

Ulrik and Anippe shared a quick look and then he looked back at the group to see what they wanted to do.

For a minute, Eli forgot he was no longer the leader and he almost spoke. He shut his mouth and turned towards Phaedra. "What do you want to do?"

She was better at masking her outrage than the rest of the group, but he knew she was offended as well given her lover was a werewolf and she was a witch. Phaedra was also a diplomat and a damn good leader and no matter how she might personally feel, she wouldn't let that get in the way of keeping up good relations with the Badawi coven.

"We graciously accept the accommodations and hospitality that you're father has extended to us." She hadn't bothered putting on a smile when she accepted their offer.

"This way please. We have cars waiting to take you to the apartments."

Everyone followed Gamal out of the airport past a bunch of taxi drivers jockeying for access to passengers in need of rides.

Willow had gotten over her distaste of the situation enough to ask questions. She caught up to walk beside their hosts. "Anippe, I'm fascinated by all things supernatural. What are the origins of your coven?"

"As far back as our family goes they have all been worshippers of Isis, the Great Lady of Magic. She is the most powerful goddess, the source and well from which we derive our power." On their walk to the vehicles that waited to take them into the city, Anippe continued to share more of their history with Willow. "We are Nubians. For generations, we lived along the Nile in Aswan. During the 1960s our families and many others were relocated to make room for the dam. Cairo is not our true home."

Once they arrived at the parking lot, Gamal gestured to a Suzuki minivan and a Skoda Roomster as their transportation. They split up and piled into the cars. Eli was sure it wasn't a coincidence that Ulrik and Anippe ended up in the same van.

He, Willow, Morgana and Mathilda ended up in the van with Gamal. It was clear Gamal felt terrible over the situation and profusely apologized once again.

"You're just the messenger, Gamal. It's okay. There are no hard feelings." Willow tried to reassure him that no one thought ill of him.

Mathilda leaned forward from the backseat, and spoke in a low voice so neither Gamal or the driver would overhear what she said. "Was I the only one that saw the sparks flying between Ulrik and Anippe? She called him Uli. After the crap some of the members of their coven believe it's clear that someone drove them apart. They're two star-crossed lovers, like Romeo and Juliet." When he looked at her she had hearts in her eyes when she spoke about the pair. Once again he was reminded she was a teenager. With all the studying and training she did, he wondered if she'd had her first crush or first kiss yet.

No one responded to her comments and she lapped into silence. He stared out the window and took in the busy, bustling streets of Cairo. Buses, cars and motorbikes were crammed onto the road. In the swarm of congested traffic, it was hard to tell if there were actual lanes or not, the way the cars switched lanes frequently and often without blinkers.

When traffic finally began to move a little quicker they were treated to the sites of old, crumbling buildings, mosques, minarets, cafes and markets. The windows at the front of the vehicle were rolled down and the sounds of the city and the blare of car horns wafted in.

Gamal turned around to address them. "You'll be staying in apartments my family own in downtown. Anything you need please do not hesitate to call us." He handed Eli a flip phone. "I've programmed my number and my sister's number into the phone... In case you are not aware, magic or witchcraft is not widely accepted or practiced here so I would avoid using it unless you absolutely have to."

No magic. Got it.

"Sure." He just hoped that somehow Killian and Katana didn't figure out where they were and show up, because if they did there would be no way they could avoid doing magic.

CHAPTER 17

Willow

THE APARTMENTS THEY were shown to were nice and entirely furnished from Ikea. Each apartment had two bedrooms. Zoriana took the other bedroom in the apartment with Eli and Willow and the others shared the second apartment. Everyone was so tired after nearly two days of travel that they said quick goodbyes to Gamal and Anippe and made plans to contact them tomorrow.

Willow realized that if each apartment only had two bedrooms, Ulrik would be relegated to sleeping on the floor. When she stepped outside to knock and find out about the sleeping arrangements that's when she saw Anippe and Ulrik down the hall. He had his arm slung over her shoulders. Guess she didn't have to worry after all, he was definitely going to be well taken care of.

It was comforting to be in a new place and know you were in the company of people that sympathized with what you were going through, had walked a mile in your shoes. She hoped that the pair would have happiness even if it was only for a few stolen moments.

In the bedroom she was sharing with Eli, she found him stretched out on the bed, fully clothed and fast asleep. He hadn't slept that well on the plane. She knew he was exhausted. She grabbed her bag and shut the door. It was the perfect time to read some of her mother's letters. Zoriana had gone in her room and shut the door. She was sure she would not be interrupted by her. After she settled on the sofa, she pulled the bundle from her bag. The letter she'd been reading on the plane was the first one she opened.

May 23, 2002

Dear Willow,

I've been in Delphi for nearly two weeks now. There has been so much to explore. The plan was to go to Egypt before heading back to the U.S., but I'm afraid that is no longer an option. We'll have to return sooner than expected. Something is going on, but I'm not exactly sure what. I have a bad feeling. Maybe it's just in my head, but

I can't shake it. There's someone I want you to meet. I'm not certain you'll get the opportunity and that makes me sad, because I think you'd like him if you did. Continue to be good for Teresa.

Love,

Mom

Many people would have ended the letter with a, 'See you soon.' Or 'Until we see each other.' Not her mother. She must have already known she would never see her again. Something in her chest hurt knowing her mother lived with the knowledge of when death would come for her. Everyone was going to die; most people didn't know the how or the when. Her mother did. For a moment, she just sat there without moving as the light faded from the sky and night descended.

Despite knowing that death loomed, her mother still chose to fall in love. She wished she'd had more time in Greece to talk with Hadrian. Her mother really cared about him. She'd wanted the two of them to meet. That was a big deal. Maybe once all of this craziness was over they could sit down and get to know one another.

***

Someone shook her awake.

"Hmm." She mumbled, still not sure what was a figment of her sleep addled brain or what was real.

"Wake up sleeping beauty." The low, sleep-tinged voice that was attempting to coax her awake sent delicious shivers up and down her spine. She smiled with her eyes still closed. "Hmm."

She could hear the smile in his voice when he responded. "Why didn't you come to bed? We both ended up sleeping in our clothes."

One eye cracked open and looked at Eli upside down. He would always be a welcome good morning. She stretched her arms above her head and stared at him.

Often when they woke up together like this, and the day was still quiet and still without a lot of noise, she had the illusion that they were just two ordinary people just living their life. They were going to wake up and prepare coffee and breakfast in the kitchen, laze about reading the newspaper on a weekend morning or kiss each other goodbye as they each headed off to work.

For a fleeting moment, she lived in that fantasy. Then reality crash landed in her lap and reminded her that a vampire was hell bent on making her his servant and possibly his bride, she was half fae and not all of her powers had manifested themselves, he was a witch that had a duty to protect her and they were not supposed to be together.

They were not here in Egypt on vacation. The mission was to find The Book of Prophecy and figure out how to defeat Killian so she didn't have to be on the run the rest of her life. She sat up and sighed.

"You okay?"

"Yeah, I'm good." She looked at him. "Let's shower, eat and figure out how to locate the book."

A couple hours later they all sat around the living room of the apartment they occupied trying to figure out the best plan for finding the book. They had the riddle The Pythia had given her which is what got them here, but now they had to determine if that was just the clue to get them to Egypt or if the Sphinx figured into all of this.

Gamal and Anippe had provided quite the breakfast spread when they showed up and things seemed cozy between her and Ulrik though they did their best to disguise their amorous looks. Clearly, her coven did not approve. Gamal didn't seem to mind. Willow returned her attention back to what was being said. It was always so easy to get caught up in other people's drama than to deal with her own.

"I think we make that the first place that we look for the book. Figure out a way to clear out tourists so there is no one in our way to look for trap doors or things like that. If that doesn't work then the Great Pyramids are there in Giza next to the Sphinx. We make those the next location to search. I believe the book is probably hidden at a high profile destination. An area that had once been a dig or excavation site." Phaedra ended the explanation to her plan. No one could argue with that logic. It made sense.

She had yet to make amends with her. For some reason she felt Phaedra probably figured it was no love lost between them. Phaedra was Eli's best friend so it was important enough to her to right things between them. Oh yeah and the teeny tiny fact of her putting her life on the line for her. Yeah, that little reason was enough to say how sorry she was for accusing her of being a megalomaniac and psychopath to boot.

Eli startled her from her thoughts. "Was there anything in your mother's letters? Did she make it to Egypt or have any clue the book was moved here?"

She shook her head and avoided everyone's eyes. Again she felt like a big disappointment, like she was letting everyone down. Why couldn't The Pythia have given her a straight answer when she asked where the book was located? Better yet, when she was having all of those retro whatever visions Eli mentioned where she was shown the past, why couldn't she have seen then where the book was moved? If only her mother had visited here, she could go to the location and see if anything called for her to touch it. Then a vision might show her what her mother saw. At least they might be that much closer to knowing something.

He must have sensed her distress because he patted her leg and kept talking. "I definitely agree that we need to clear everyone out if we can." He looked at Gamal. "I know you mentioned not using magic if we don't have to, but in case it's at the Sphinx and we have to resort to magic, it would be helpful not to have a bunch of tourists in our way."

"What kind of excuses can be made to have it closed?" Ulrik asked.

"It's not just the Sphinx you have to worry about the whole area is usually ripe with tourists on any given day. The area to be closed off would need to be much bigger." He rubbed his chin and pondered ways to cordon off the area. "Let me make a couple phone calls." As he stepped outside the apartment he was already talking rapid Arabic with someone on the phone.

This was all starting to feel like Greece all over again. They had no clues or definite ideas. Essentially they were looking for a needle in a haystack. She wanted to scream she was so frustrated. When she happened to look up, Max was staring at her. He gave her a small smile and motioned for her to meet him outside. She nodded. She could feel both Eli's and Phaedra's eyes follow them out the door.

Max leaned his arms on the railing of the balcony. "Pretty serious stuff."

"Yep." She avoided his gaze. Sometimes she forgot how well he knew her and how well he was tuned into her emotions.

"It's okay to feel helpless, Willow." He spoke the words softly. Over the past few months she'd grown accustomed to him providing comic relief, she forgot how insightful he could be. "It's okay to feel anger, frustration."

"I miss the days when you couldn't talk." A mirthless chuckle escaped as she dabbed leaky eyes and looked out on the rooftops of the nearby buildings.

"Ever since everything with Eli you've been keeping everything so bottled up. You're upset with yourself for not being able to save Eli, upset over not being more helpful in finding this book... L.I.G."

Genuinely, she laughed this time. He came over and vigorously rubbed up and down her arms.

"Just let it go?" She laughed harder this time. "Let it all go, huh?"

"Yep. It's everyone's job to figure this out. Don't feel like you have to take on anything alone."

She hugged him. He always had this calming effect on her. If there was one thing she was glad for it was that. He might not be her dog anymore, but he was still her friend. "Thank you." It came out muffled because she was pressed against his chest.

After a few more minutes outside they walked back into the apartment. Eli looked at her with a question on his face. She gave him a smile and went and sat beside him on the floor. He leaned into her. "You okay?"

"Yeah." She kissed him on the cheek.

CHAPTER 18

Eli

WHEN WILLOW RETURNED after her talk with Max she seemed more herself. He liked that they had a strong bond. He wrapped his arm around her. Whatever had been weighing on her had been removed. He could see it on her face. If only the issues that plagued him could be resolved with only a talk.

Part of him felt a little relieved that Gamal had asked them to limit their use of magic in public spaces. He had to admit he was feeling a little uncertain about his performance right now. The thought of someone needing to count on him or depend on him for his magic had him second-guessing himself. His magic wouldn't be as powerful as it once was and he didn't want to be the reason someone got hurt. If he only had to use his fighting skills he felt secure in taking on any attack or enemy, but knew he had to get his confidence back up when it came to magic or he was useless to them.

While they waited for Gamal to come back with information, Morgana and Mathilda walked across the hall to their apartment.

A short while later, Gamal came back. He slapped his phone against his thigh and looked a bit sheepish. "My father wants to meet all of you before he deals with having the Sphinx and Pyramids shut down."

Phaedra stood. "We are happy to meet with your father if it means accomplishing what we came here to do." She tried to appear diplomatic and levelheaded, but he knew her blood was boiling. If the man had met with them to begin with, as intended, they wouldn't be sitting on their hands now.

"I will have the vans brought around so we can head to the coven." Gamal left again.

"I apologize that things have been so crazy since your arrival." Anippe addressed everyone. "There is always politics here when it comes to getting anything done. It is not my father's way, but there are some in our coven that would rather see themselves making the decisions so he must jump through hoops to keep everyone happy."

He understood all too well how that worked.

"Thank you, Anippe. We appreciate your father doing his best to accommodate us." Phaedra gave the girl a genuine smile. Anippe smiled and returned to Ulrik's side.

Eli knew this meeting was going to be anything but pleasant, especially since Gamal and Anippe had already mentioned some of the members of the coven didn't like the fact that he and Willow were together.

Mathilda and Morgana returned and went to stand by Ulrik and Anippe. "Are you okay?" Ulrik leaned towards Mathilda with a concerned look.

"Yes... why?" Mathilda leaned away from him and looked annoyed at him invading her body space.

"Your eyes look strange." He stared into her eyes and kept getting closer.

"I'm fine." She moved away from him clearly creeped out and sat on the floor.

That was peculiar. He'd have to ask Ulrik about that later. Should he be concerned about something going on with Mathilda? He never figured her for a pill popper or any other sort of drugs, although drug use might explain her out of character behavior of holding a grudge for this long. He glanced over at her and watched her talk to Phaedra. No. He couldn't see her doing that. Not much longer after that Gamal came back for them.

The drive to the coven took them to the affluent neighborhood of Heliopolis. They passed luxury hotels, swanky restaurants and upscale shopping centers before they arrived to the residential section. The houses were on a grandiose level and sat behind security gates.

The house they pulled up to was similar to the other homes in the neighborhood: terra cotta colored stucco with Roman motif ornamentation made of gypsum plaster. The house was three stories tall and even had a small spire on one side.

"I think I should remain out here. My presence won't help your case, and I don't wish to hurt your chances of getting what you need."

Eli hated the idea of kowtowing to some people especially these idiots that were offended by his and Willow's relationship. On this occasion, he was glad it was Phaedra calling the shots because he would have brought Ulrik in the house just to piss them off.

"Thanks for being considerate Ulrik, maybe it is best you wait outside."

"I'll keep you company... we can take a walk." Anippe jumped at the opportunity to spend some time alone with Ulrik. The two walked off down the street before they made it to the door.

The door had a huge bronze door knocker that was a replica of the goddess Isis, with her wings spread out on either side of her and a solar disk with cow's horns sat on top of her head. Like most coven doors there was no keyhole. Gamal pulled out a key and the keyhole appeared. When he placed the key inside it turned on its own and the door opened.

Gamal did a quick about face. "Please remove your shoes before entering." He kicked off his shoes and left them by the door. They all followed suit.

When they stepped inside the décor consisted of deep jewel tones. There was no time to see anything other than the living room because off the side of the foyer they were led into a room that had a long wooden table that sat low to the ground. Floor cushions surrounded the table on all sides.

"Please have a seat. My father and some of the members will be here shortly." Gamal left them to get situated while he went in search of his father. Eli sat in between Willow and Phaedra.

A woman came into the room carrying a tray. "I have brought you some Shai while you wait." For a moment he wished he'd done some research on common words so he knew what Shai was.

The little glasses she sat down in front of each of them had a hot, brown colored liquid in it. He picked it up and took a sip.

Tea.

He took another sip. It was really good tea.

Gamal entered the room. "My father and some of the Elders are going to dine with you. A meal has been prepared for your arrival." He glanced towards the door and then turned back to them and dropped his voice. "A few tips on dining with Egyptians." Everyone leaned in to listen. "Let my father or one of the Elders serve you, do not serve yourself. Second, we eat mostly with our hands, but do not use or eat with your left hand. It's considered unhygienic..." He looked upwards for a few seconds like he was trying to remember everything he needed them to remember before his father and the Elders arrived. "Oh yes, and don't ask for salt... and also don't ask how the food was made."

Just as he finished up an older, portly man with a beard entered the room. The galabeya, a long-sleeved, floor length tunic he wore, was pristine white. Two other men, similarly dressed, but skinnier and beardless, and a woman wearing a flowing skirt and blouse followed him. They sat on the remaining cushions at the table.

"My name is Bakari. I am the head of the Badawi coven." The portly man introduced himself. "These are some of the Elders: Kek, Sabra and Fukayna."

Once the introductions were out of the way dishes were delivered to the table. Eli knew the falafel dish as soon as it came to the table, but some of the other dishes he wasn't sure about. Gamal wasted no time in filling them in on the names of the delectable dishes that came to the table.

"That is mahshi." He pointed at a dish of red and green bell peppers stuffed with a rice mixture. "That stew is called molokhia. Those green bits are chopped up leafy greens and there is chicken, coriander and garlic." Everything smelled delicious. "That dish is fattah. On the bottom is rice and some crispy bread, then you have a tomato sauce and beef."

He took his seat. "For dessert we'll be having konafa. I'll explain what it is once it's served... Eat up."

Maybe this meeting wouldn't go as bad as he originally assumed, they were being served a meal. The thought had just barely passed through his mind when Kek, who had yet to serve himself or anyone else spoke. "So you are the Oracle." He said it as a statement and not a question as he looked at Willow dubiously.

"Yes." She smiled at the man. Eli could tell she hadn't caught the man's tone.

Kek's eyes cut to Eli. For long, tense seconds they both eyed each other. Eli was trying not to be disrespectful or rude since he was a guest and no longer the leader of The Protectors, but this guy was starting to piss him off. It's like he wanted to start something just so he could have a reason to make sure Bakari said no to them.

"Kek, let them eat their food in peace. We show our guests hospitality when they come here. There will be time enough for questions after the meal." Bakari didn't even look up from his plate of food when he spoke.

It took Kek a minute, but eventually he dished food onto his plate and ate in sullen silence.

"How are you enjoying Cairo so far?" Fukayna asked with a smile.

Willow, Mathilda, Zoriana and Morgana started making small talk with Fukayna.

Every now and then, Eli's eyes would wander to Kek. The man picked at his food. Annoyance sat on Kek's face like he'd eaten something bad. Sabra had yet to say anything other than hello. He was engrossed in his food.

Eli knew they were literally on a countdown before the shit hit the fan. This guy wasn't going to just let this go. Twenty minutes later, Kek exploded just like he thought he would. "Nope. I'm not going to do it. I won't just sit here and pretend to have a nice meal with these... these, this criminal." He spat out and then threw his napkin onto the table.

Eli glared at him. Kek's angry stare didn't waver. For seconds there was only silence.

"You break the law and then come begging for our help..."

"And I answered for that." He bit out.

"Yet here you sit... with her." Kek sneered at him. "Thumbing your nose at us. How disrespectful of you to come here and ask for our help when you know this is wrong..."

Eli stood. "I'm not hungry anymore." He was seething. There was so much more he wanted to say, but he didn't want to give this man the satisfaction.

"Please, please, just sit..." Bakari gave Kek a dirty look, but it didn't make him back down.

Phaedra spoke up. "Maybe it's best if we go." She placed her napkin on the table and stood. "We were told when we arrived that there were issues. We're just here to locate something of importance. Gamal stated that we needed your permission... You asked us here so we came. We're trying our best to be respectful in your coven, in your country..."

Kek interrupted her. "Respect? What do you know of respect? You bring this half breed in here..." He jabs his finger at Willow. "That's showing us respect?"

Eli had had enough. If he stayed one minute longer he was going to leap across the table and beat the guy within an inch of his life. 'Come on Willow let's go." Ulrik had the right idea not setting foot in this place. Their group started to get up from the table.

Sabra, Fukayna and Kek began arguing in Arabic.

Bakari followed them outside. He slightly wheezed as he tried to catch up with Phaedra. "Please... forgive... the bad behavior."

Phaedra stopped so the man wouldn't over exert himself trying to catch her. "I apologize for the insults you suffered in there." He looked directly at Willow that time. She was doing her best to appear unfazed, but he knew Kek's comments hurt her.

"That is not our way and I am embarrassed it happened." The man wrung his hands. "What was it you said you needed again?"

Gamal spoke up. "They need access to the Sphinx and the Pyramid without the worry of tourists."

Bakari nodded. "Yes, I will make some phone calls. Please... let me make amends for what happened." He pleaded with Phaedra.

"Thank you. We appreciate that." Her gracious manner lit up Bakari's face.

"Okay. I will go take care of that and call Gamal when it is done." He scurried back inside the house.

"I'm so sorry that happened." Gamal looked appalled and embarrassed. Bright red blotches could be seen in the warm brown on the skin of his cheeks. Eli wasn't sure because of embarrassment, anger or a mixture of both.

"You don't have to apologize for other people's stupid behavior." Morgana consoled him.

"You okay?" Eli pulled Willow close. She nodded, but she wouldn't look at him. He lifted her chin so she would have to look at him. "Don't let what that asshat said to you get to you okay." The word 'asshat' made her grin. "He's just a small-minded bigot." He was glad he made her smile. Leaning in, he pecked her on the lips.

Bakari must have really felt bad about what happened over lunch because they were ten minutes away from the apartments when Gamal got the call. He had the drivers change route to head in the direction of the Sphinx and the Pyramids.

The energy in the vehicle changed. Everyone seemed to be excited that they might finally find The Book of Prophecy. Willow was practically jumping in her seat with excitement.

It didn't take them long to get there. As promised, whomever Bakari talked to had it cleared out. There were no tourists. In fact, no one was at the Sphinx or anywhere within the vicinity. The place was completely deserted. He wondered how that had gone down with the tourists being told they had to leave. What excuse had they used?

He couldn't put too much thought into that right now. They got out of the vans and stood around trying to decide what should happen first.

"Let's split into groups and walk around the statue. Look for anything that might lead to some hidden access: a button, lever, anything. Or if you see an area where someone could have hidden anything." Phaedra laid out the game plan. Everyone broke off into groups of twos or threes.

"Please remember to be gentle. It is a piece of history." Gamal called out to everyone's back as they headed towards the statue.

His eyes wandered to the human face missing a nose before it raked over the lion body. Considering the myriad of supernatural beings that existed in the modern world he wondered if there had ever been a living, breathing Sphinx.

"Do you think we'll find it here?" Willow looked up at the statue as she asked the question.

"I don't know, baby."

For the next forty-five minutes, they poked and prodded the base of the statue hoping to find a trapdoor, access panel or hidden compartment that held The Book of Prophecy, but nothing.

"I don't think it's here." Willow said breathlessly, like she'd been running a marathon. She was disappointed.

Phaedra looked up at the sky. The light was beginning to fade from the day. "Let's head over to the pyramids and see if there is anything there before it gets dark."

Without hesitation, everyone rushed towards the pyramids. There were three in total. "We'll take the Great Pyramid." Max called out as he jogged towards the largest of the three pyramids.

"We'll take the Pyramid of Khafre." Anippe shouted and Gamal and Ulrik followed her in that direction.

"Okay..." He had no idea the name of the last pyramid. "We'll take the last one."

"Meet back at the Sphinx." Phaedra yelled so her voice would carry over the distance.

Great.

He realized they'd been left with the pyramid that was the farthest away. They couldn't lose the light. Since there was no one around to see him use magic, what was the harm? "Give me your hand."

Willow looked over at him, out of breath with sweat on her brow. "What?"

He stopped running. "Give me your hand."

She stopped and gave him her hand. Once she did, he teleported them closer.

"I thought…" She began.

"We don't want to lose the light, right?" He winked and gave her a sly grin. She smirked.

They split up and each walked in a different direction around the pyramid. With the light waning, he wanted to make sure they had sufficient time to make it around the pyramid at least once before they had to call it. No matter how much he jabbed his hands and fingers here and there, into cracks, crevices or openings, nothing gave way or opened. He was beginning to believe they were about to hit another dead end. There hadn't been any loud barks of discovery from any of the other groups either.

Time had slipped away from him, but by the time he looked up again, he could see he and Willow now explored the same side of the pyramid. As they drew closer, he saw the crestfallen look she wore. She shook her head once they stood side by side. "Nothing."

It was certainly disappointing, but it had to be here somewhere in Egypt. They would find it. "Let's rejoin the others." He took her hand and teleported them back to the Sphinx."

CHAPTER 19

Willow

AFTER THE SEARCH yesterday at the Sphinx and the pyramids yielded nothing she had to admit she was feeling a little annoyed. How many other landmarks were they going to have to search. Today they were headed to Saqqara. She hadn't felt a connection to anything she came in contact with. There was no pull or tug towards anything. Max was right though, she was grateful she didn't have to do this alone. Having the Protectors with her did make this easier.

It was early. She'd been unable to sleep any longer. The balcony off their bedroom had a magnificent view of the city. She stood out there in one of Eli's t-shirts and bare feet. Her eyes were focused on the skyline. The sun was beginning to rise and she wished she'd brought her guitar along on the trip. Being so engulfed in all of this had kept her from her music. She'd never gone this long without playing or singing. It was partly what kept her sane. Her finger began to tap out a rhythm on the balcony railing and then she started to hum. Then the tune of the song took shape in her head and she started singing to herself, trying to keep it low so she wouldn't wake him.

It was freeing and comforting to sing. She realized she was singing The Cures 'Lovesong' and she couldn't contain the small smile that lit up her face. Suddenly, arms surrounded her and pulled her close. The brief jolt of shock dissipated the second she realized it was Eli. "Keep singing babe." He whispered sleepily into her ear as he held her against his body. She could feel him nuzzling her neck.

She resumed singing and sang a little louder for his benefit. When she finished he kissed her shoulder and smiled into her skin. "You like that song, don't you?"

"It makes me think of you." As they stood there together, silent, she wondered what he was thinking, feeling, but she didn't ask.

The sun climbed up the sky, bathing the day in a beautiful light. He held her tighter and kissed the top of her head. "I love you." The words held such tenderness to them.

She placed her hand on his arm. "I love you too." For a while they just stayed locked together. The moments like this are what gave her strength to keep fighting. This is what she was fighting for... more moments like this one, a lifetime of moments like this one. They had to find that book.

Once thoughts of The Book of Prophecy encroached upon her solitude she knew their moment was over. "Let's shower and get the others up so we can get going."

He kissed the side of her face and they went back into their room. After she showered and dressed she went across to the other apartment. She held up her fist to knock, but her hand hovered there in the air for a minute. Her nerves were rattling her. She pushed the feeling away and knocked on the door. A few seconds later, Phaedra opened the door.

"Hi."

"Hi." Phaedra responded. It wasn't unwelcoming, but it wasn't inviting either. As a matter of fact, she stood in the doorway and hadn't asked her to come inside.

"Can we talk... out here?" Willow didn't want anyone eavesdropping on their conversation. She realized how hypocritical it was of her to want privacy when she so often wanted and had listened in on conversations.

Phaedra stepped out into the hallway and shut the door behind her. She crossed her arms over her chest and stood staring at Willow with a blank expression.

She's not going to make this easy.

Willow swallowed and squared her shoulders. "Listen, the day everything happened with Eli... I said some awful things that I didn't mean..."

"Yes, you did." Phaedra interrupted her, but there was still no emotion to her words.

"Well they were said in the heat of anger, that doesn't mean that I really feel that way about you..." Now she sounded defensive. "What I'm trying to say is I'm sorry... I haven't gotten to know you like I've gotten to know the others... and yesterday when you stuck up for me with Kek... Thank you for that..." She faltered and looked away for a second before looking at Phaedra's face once more. "I realized I was so very wrong about you... I don't know why we haven't become friends yet, but I would like to try."

It took nearly a minute before Phaedra responded. "Apology accepted." She went to walk back into the apartment.

"Wait. What about everything else I said?" Willow was trying not to look shocked.

"We're not going to become besties over night. Things will happen the way they're supposed to." She offered up a smile that included raised eyebrows that seemed to be asking if this was over.

"Okay." Once she said the word, Phaedra went into the apartment and shut the door. Guess that's the best she was going to get. At least she'd finally apologized like she should have right after it happened.

***

Gamal, Anippe and Ulrik arrived and they piled into the vans to head to Saqqara. It was the only place they had scheduled to search today. It was a bit of a process getting these places closed to the public so they could have their privacy. She couldn't imagine how many looks and stares they would receive from people watching them poke around.

The ancient burial ground was deserted when they arrived. The day was still and no air or breeze seemed to whip around, which made the day even hotter. She wiped sweat from her brow as they spread out to begin the hunt. Besides the Djoser's step pyramid there were ruins of the burial ground complex that had been excavated and preserved. They had quite a bit of ground to cover considering how many possible hiding places the complex offered.

They started with the pyramid and covered every area leading all the way up to the top. Examining every step for potential trapdoors and compartments that might unearth the book. In the hot sun with no shade, it was a grueling, sweaty process. Her fingers were caked with dirt from running them through the sand and earth.

It had taken over an hour to search the pyramid from top to bottom and now they needed to search the burial complex, which consisted of a lot of different areas. At this point they split into groups so they could cover more of the area quickly. She drank down the cold bottle of water Anippe and Gamal offered. They'd been thoughtful enough to pack a cooler full of cold water.

She ended up with Ulrik as a partner during the search of the ruins. They walked in silence under the roofed colonnade entrance that led into the complex. It was the first time she'd been somewhat alone with Ulrik. She ran her fingers along the stone pillars as they passed, wishing she felt some pull or connection to the building. Unfortunately, there was no voice beckoning her in a certain direction or an imaginary string that seemed to tether her to any place within the ruins. It was hard not to feel that they probably wouldn't find the book here either.

She was deep in her own thoughts when his voice pulled her out of her head.

"You and Eli... was it easy for you to become lovers?" He looked her in the eyes as they walked.

The direct question was unexpected. She looked away and mulled over his words. She was sure the road to where they were now hadn't been easy. "No, it wasn't easy." She mused over Eli's strong sense of duty that kept them apart. "Nope... When I finally professed my feelings, he wasn't ready." Her gaze returned to his. "It broke my heart."

They lapsed into silence once again as the long walk along the corridor ended and they found themselves in a hall that once held floor to ceiling columns.

In between each column, on either side, were smaller chambers. The search of this hall alone could take quite a bit of time.

"You take the left hand side and I'll take the right hand side." He suggested. She appreciated that he offered it as a way for them to work without making it seem like his was the only way. Since it made sense she nodded and stepped to the left. She got right to work, feeling along the walls and columns before she entered the first chamber.

After searching the first chamber she came out to repeat the process of pushing, poking and prodding the wall and a column before she entered the next chamber. She'd completed this process about four times when Ulrik spoke again. "You both inspire me." He said the words while his fingers worked along a column, probing for a secret hideaway. Willow stopped what she was doing. "Since I've met you and seen the two of you together I am awestruck, which hasn't happened in a long time. When you've been around as long as I have, you've pretty much seen everything. Nothing surprises you anymore." He turned to her.

She was shocked by his confession.

"Surely, you've noticed there is more between Anippe and I than friendship."

She wasn't sure if he was looking for an answer because it didn't exactly sound like a question, but she nodded.

"When I came here after being excommunicated I had no expectations." While he spoke it seemed like his mind had drifted back to that time in his life. "I was never a man that had known true love and had figured that was something that wasn't meant to be." A large smile, like someone had awakened the sun transformed Ulrik's face. "It wasn't love at first sight, but what I felt for Anippe as I got to know her grew into a deep, passionate love for both of us." As quickly as the smile was there, it was snuffed out by some dark memory.

"What happened?" She asked quietly, afraid that maybe she should have waited to let him speak again.

Sad eyes stared at her. It was several seconds before he responded. "Many in her coven were appalled by our relationship. I didn't find this out until I sought Bakari's permission for her hand in marriage..."

It was hard to keep the shock off her face. She could tell the two were in love, but hadn't realized things had been that serious between the two.

"There were threats against me at first, which I could handle... but when members of her own coven threatened to strip her of her magic..." His gaze flicked towards Willow almost in an apologetic way. "When they threatened this thing... and said she would be forced from her homeland as well if we went through with the wedding, I could not go through with it."

What he'd just told her made her so angry she wanted to go and beat Kek and whoever else had threatened the pair to a pulp. She was sure it had been the vile man from lunch that led the angry mob with pitchforks.

"I never told her about the threats that had been made. I just left..." The pain in his eyes was haunting. "I'd been doomed to a life alone with no community. I would not condemn her to that." He went back to his search and for a moment she thought that was the end of it, but then he spoke as he worked. "Then I saw you and Eli together..."

She was rooted to the spot, listening to what he was going to say.

"I saw the love between the two of you and I thought they have not had to face adversity yet. One of them will crack like I did when faced with overcoming the people that don't want to see them together." Ulrik stopped again, but didn't turn towards her. "When I heard that Eli had gone through with the stripping because he chose to love you no matter what anyone said, no matter the perverse law... I felt shame. For the first time in probably hundreds of years, I was ashamed at how easily I let others keep me from love out of fear."

Her thoughts went back to that night when he and Phaedra had dragged an unconscious Eli into the living room and how Ulrik had said he was an honorable man.

"I've decided that if Anippe will have me, I vow I will not let her go this time. I'm prepared to make any sacrifice for us to be together." When he turned back to her this time, she could see the grin that broke out on his face and it made her smile.

"I think that's amazing. You both deserve to be happy. I'm glad you're going to get that." For some reason, she found herself embracing him in a hug. He hugged her back.

"Thank you." He was beaming.

They went back to their search, both smiling and happy, lost in thoughts of the ones they loved. She was flattered by his admiration over how she and Eli loved one another. It made her want to fight that much harder to find this book and defeat Killian so she could spend the rest of her life in peace, loving him.

CHAPTER 20

Eli

EVERYONE WAS EXHAUSTED. They'd searched the Sphinx, the Great Pyramids and Saqqara and hadn't found the book yet. Their steps were heavy as they trudged into the apartment. Anxiety was rolling off everyone in waves.

Where is this damn book?

Eli ran his hands through his hair in annoyance before he dropped onto the sofa. It had been a long couple of days between the constant searching and the run in with the anti-hybrid group. Willow collapsed next to him and rested her head on his shoulder.

Quiet contemplation was happening around the room when Mathilda spoke up. "Are you guys ready to listen to me yet?" She implored them with her hands on her hips.

"Remind us what your theory was again?" Phaedra was a bit exasperated with the fruitless search so far as they all were.

"It was too easy to think The Pythia was pointing Willow in the direction of the Sphinx. It's so on the nose. I don't think Phaedra is wrong in that it's being hidden at a prominent site, that site just isn't here in Cairo..." She looked around at all of them. "When the Sphinx gives Oedipus that riddle to solve he'd been on the road headed to Thebes. Thebes is now modern day Luxor. I think the Book of Prophecy is in the Valley of the Kings."

Eli looked around at everyone to see if they were making the same connection Mathilda was. Some of them looked skeptical that she could be right.

"You guys, Oedipus was a Greek King traveling to Egypt and headed to Thebes, which is now Luxor where the Valley of the Kings is located. It makes sense The Pythia would have used this to point us in the right direction. Can't you see the connection?"

When she said it like that. It did make sense. Willow was nodding her head and excited at the new idea. What did they have to lose? They'd searched so many other places and had yet to find the book.

Anippe looked at her watch. "Luxor is a little over five hundred kilometers away. It's late. The next train won't leave for Luxor until the morning, but that way will be slow. By plane would be the quickest route."

"I think I know someone that may be able to help us out. He has a private plane that could get us there if someone hasn't chartered it." Ulrik offered. Eli was starting to be thankful he'd agreed to let the Dane tag along.

Ulrik went to the landline phone in the apartment and dialed a number. When someone picked up on the other end, he spoke French.

Eli hoped Mathilda's theory was right so they could finally get this book and start dealing with the real issue, which was how they were going to defeat Killian. Although it was necessary they be on this scavenger hunt for the book so it didn't fall into Killian's hands, it was aggravating how difficult it had been.

It didn't help that the whole anti-hybrid and anti-mixing of the supernatural factions was now an issue that kept rearing its ugly head. They had enough to deal with already. He didn't want something else added to the list.

He shut his eyes for a second, needing to rest and clear his mind. They'd been on autopilot since they arrived in Egypt and it felt like ages since he'd meditated.

Ulrik hung up the phone. "We are to be at terminal hall four at Cairo International Airport in two hours."

Good. He was glad they wouldn't have to wait until tomorrow to get to Luxor.

"Okay everyone, grab your stuff. If this book is in the Valley of the Kings like Mathilda says it is we won't be coming back here. We'll head straight to the airport." Phaedra issued the order.

Eli kept his eyes closed for a moment longer. All he could think was:

Please let us find this so we can go home.

When they arrived and boarded the Gulfstream G550 in the private hall of the airport he saw the expression on Willow's face change to one of giddiness. "I can't believe I'm on a private jet." She whispered to him excitedly as she took in the interior.

It was nice to see this side of her. It was one of the things about her that had first attracted him, her enthusiasm about things. To see her face lit up and so animated warmed his heart.

"Dude, we're on a G5." Max leaned across the aisle. It seemed Willow's excitement about the plane was catching.

"I know." Willow leaned across his lap to gush to Max about them being on a G5.

"Do you think Ulrik can get him to fly us back to Salem in this thing?"

Eli looked at Phaedra and smiled before he shook his head. "Max, why don't you take my seat and I'll take yours."

Max agreed and kept chattering with Willow as they made the change. It wasn't long before Mathilda, Morgana, Gamal and Anippe joined in the discussion. Then they were up out of their seats exploring the back of the aircraft.

"There's champagne back here." Max could be heard saying. Next thing they knew the cork was being popped. Phaedra was about to head to the back to stop the shenanigans.

Eli put his hand on her leg to stop her. "Let them have their fun." He listened to the tinkling sound of Willow's laughter and the sound of them toasting with the champagne flutes. A tired smile crossed his face. "You and I both know if we find that book tonight we head back to Salem and it's more hardcore training to get her prepared to go up against Killian who we still have to locate. This doesn't end tonight. It's really just the beginning."

Phaedra pursed her lips together and nodded.

The two of them were such realists it was hard to allow themselves to just have fun and be in the moment when they knew the hardest fight was yet to come.

Zoriana joined in the fun and had a small sip of champagne. Eli was glad to see her doing something other than sulking.

Ulrik dropped down in the seat in front of them. "No celebration for the two of you?"

They both shook their heads.

"Thanks again for making this happen." Phaedra told the Dane.

"No big deal. I was happy to help." The three of them lapsed into a comfortable silence. When Eli looked up again he could tell that Ulrik was watching Anippe. He felt bad for the Dane. What was his excuse for not taking the love that he wanted? What had frightened him away from being with the one he loved and truly being happy?

The three-hour flight went by fairly quickly. Even though Gamal had joined in the fun onboard the flight, he'd also used the three hours headed to Luxor to call in a favor. He had a friend who was an operator at the Valley of the Kings. His friend had agreed to give them entrance once they arrived, even though it was after the last tour had been completed. At least with all the tourists gone if they were ambushed they didn't have to worry about any humans being casualties or seeing them use magic.

In the daytime the site probably wasn't as unsettling as it was in the dark. Despite the use of flashlights it was an eerie place when you remembered that it was a burial site. The night air in the desert had a slight chill to it. They'd decided to split off into groups to search the different tombs. That way they could cut down on their search time and get out of the place that much faster. Willow shivered. He took off his jacket and draped it around her.

"Thank you." She put her arms through the sleeves and rolled them up.

Apparently, Gamal's friend had been unaware of the security team that patrolled the site. Two men walked towards them speaking in Arabic, the beam of their flashlights shining onto their faces as they cautiously approached them. "Ma aldhy tafealuh huna?"

Gamal took charge. "We'll handle this. Head into the tombs and meet back here when you find something. Cell phones won't work well out here and won't work at all underground so if something happens get out as soon as you can."

They hesitated. The idea of the two getting into serious trouble for helping them out didn't sit well with anyone.

"Go." Gamal urged them and then he and Anippe rushed off to deal with the security.

They were here now. Better try and use what little time they might have to find the elusive book. "Be safe everyone and meet back here as soon as you can." Phaedra told them.

Willow, Max and Mathilda went off in one direction. Phaedra and Zoriana in another, which left him with Ulrik and Morgana. He shined his flashlight on the placard at the tomb entrance: Pharoah Thutmose III (KV34).

The tomb wasn't that well lit. The beams from their flashlights gave them glimpses of the cavernous space. The tomb slipped further into darkness the lower they went. If their flashlights did go out he could always use magic to illuminate the chamber. With more light the tomb was probably impressive, but they weren't here to sightsee.

Without saying anything they fanned out to look for the book. They'd been searching the tomb for nearly a half an hour when he heard one of them coming up behind him. He thought it was Ulrik and remembered he was going to ask him about the incident with Mathilda.

"Ulrik, I meant to ask you, what was up earlier when you asked Mathilda about her eyes. Should I be worried?"

No one said anything.

"Ulrik?" He went to turn around and ask the question again when he took a blow to the back of the head and passed out.

CHAPTER 21

Willow

AS THE THREE of them descended down into Ramses VI tomb no flashlights were needed because the pathway was lit. Murals and hieroglyphics covered the ceilings and every inch of wall space. It didn't matter that in places they were discolored, faded and crumbling. The fact that most of it had withstood time was a testament of itself. Archaeologists had taken great care to preserve what was left of the mighty Pharoah's tomb, despite the grave robbers that had looted and plundered the space of any treasures. It was hard not to be struck by how amazing the tomb was, to still be intact after all this time.

She was fascinated with it all and wished again she was here as a tourist and not hunting for an ancient book, but the descent didn't quell her anxiety about the fact that they were in a grave, a very large grave.

Can't believe these guys used to bury their whole households with them.

She shuddered. Only narcissists and tyrants would want to make sure they were being waited on hand and foot in the afterlife.

The long walk down to the burial chamber finally ended. "Let's separate and look around. See if we find anything." Mathilda's suggestion was met with agreement from her and Max. Each of them went in different directions.

It has to be here somewhere.

The closer she walked to the back of the chamber the more she felt a pull nearly identical to the magnetic pull she'd felt at the ruins in Greece. The book had to be here somewhere. There wasn't a ton of space where something could be hidden, unless... she looked around at the walls. Maybe there was a lever or button that if pushed or pulled would reveal a hiding space. She just had to locate it. For a second she hesitated, fingerprints on these ancient walls might not be good. Unfortunately, she couldn't worry about that right now. She had to find that book. Plus, she wanted to get out of this place. People were buried down here and it was kind of giving her the creeps.

She worked her way around the room pressing here and there and looking for any areas where there might be notches or open spaces. Twenty minutes later, she pushed on a piece of wall and fell forward into another chamber. This room was dark. She pulled the flashlight from her waistband. When she shined the light around, she saw that the room was no bigger than a closet. Maybe there was once treasure stored here, but no longer was that the case. Cobwebs filled the corners and she nearly choked on the dust that clogged the air.

She braced herself on her arms to push herself to her feet and part of the floor rolled out from under her. A scream was about to erupt from her throat when she thought she was about to fall into a hole, but it was merely a hidey-hole of sorts. Something was wrapped in a tarp and laid in the space that was about a foot deep. All she could do was stare at it for several moments in shocked silence. With trembling fingers she reached down to retrieve it. The tarp fell away as she picked up the heavy object and revealed the edge of an old, worn leather bound tome. She coughed when a dust cloud rose up smacking her in the face. Sputtering, she waved her hand in front of her face trying to clear the dust away.

Once she was no longer choking she removed the rest of the tarp and saw the book had writing on the cover. She couldn't read the title because it was written in Greek, but she knew in her heart of hearts that what she held was The Book of Prophecy. Along with the Greek title was a keyhole. Her finger traced over the irregular looking keyhole. Where was the key? She leaned over and looked back into the hole she'd just removed the book from. When her eyes didn't instantly land on something she put her free hand in the hole and felt around. Nothing. She would take the victory for the day. They had the book. She could worry about the key later.

Mathilda was going to be so happy she'd been right. Her face was going to light up when she saw the book.

Willow stood and held it tightly to her chest as she left the chamber, but more dust swirled in the air around her. Coughing, she walked the path back to find Max and Mathilda. She put her hand in Eli's jacket pocket searching for tissue to cover her nose. Something dropped against the ground and made a clinking noise when she pulled out the tissues. When she looked down she realized it must have come from Eli's jacket pocket. She bent to pick it up and saw it was part of a locket. The moment her fingers touched the golden piece of the locket, the inner voice that always sounded before she had a vision spoke, 'Show me.'

The elements swirled and moved around her and then she stood in Killian's throne room. She'd been in here too many times in her dreams not to know exactly where she was. Who owned the locket and how had Eli come to have it?

She focused back on what was going on in the room. Killian sat on his throne and Katana had just walked into the room. It struck her that this time she could actually hear. Katana's footsteps echoed off the marble floor as she approached.

Was it possible the more often she experienced these visions, all of her senses would be used or would it be a random occurrence for her to hear visions? There was still so much to learn.

Katana stopped and knelt before Killian.

"You have failed." His voice was cold and unforgiving.

"I didn't, the witch betrayed us." Katana said equally as cold. She was not frightened of Killian's wrath in the least. She was upset. This was good news though, if the witch that had been working with them betrayed them, then maybe this meant he or she had a change of heart.

"Do you want me to find her and bring her to you?" Katana looked fierce. Willow loathed that Katana was merely an extension of Killian. She was always willing and ready to do anything for Killian.

"Yes, bring Morgana to me."

The moment she heard Killian say Morgana's name she came out of her trance with a jolt of shock. Her breathing was erratic and bordered on hyperventilating for the several seconds afterwards. She was horrified and about to call for help when her vision adjusted. Whatever she was about to say died on her lips as she took in the scene before her.

Morgana stood in the center of the tomb looking like an evil sorceress instead of the cute, agreeable sprite she'd come to think of her as. How she'd managed to hide the naked malevolent look that now gleamed in her eyes for all these years Willow didn't know. Here was the real psychopath. Something twisted in her gut to know that Morgana had betrayed them all.

Those thoughts were short lived when she realized Morgana wasn't alone. Morgana was using magic to keep Mathilda held aloft against the wall. The girl had no control over her own body. She was positioned like Jesus hanging on the cross. Tears trickled down her face.

Max was in the corner. "Max." She rushed forward clutching the book when she realized he was hurt.

"Uh uh. Stay where you are. He's fine for now." Even Morgana's voice sounded different: darker, edgier, full of malice.

"He's hurt." The silver net she'd seen that day at Samson's supernatural weapon warehouse had Max penned to the ground. He was in his human form, but he was naked. At some point he must have changed into his wolf form, but when the silver started burning his skin he changed back.

He whimpered like a dog and she knew he was in pain.

"Just please, let me..." She tried to get to him again, when Morgana pulled a customized gun from her bag and fired a shot at Max. The gunshot had no sound. There must have been some sort of silencer on the gun. The shot hit him in the shoulder. He howled and yelped in distress. She didn't have to be a rocket scientist to know they were silver bullets.

"Now are we going to have any more problems with you listening to my instructions?" She put the gun away and eyed Willow.

All Willow could do was shake her head no. She took a step back and stumbled, resulting in her landing on her butt in the dirt. She still held the heavy book in her hands.

"Eli! Eli!" She knew they were somewhere in another tomb, but she had to try and call for help. When that didn't seem to be working she tried to call out to him telepathically. 'ELI! ELI!' No response. Something was wrong.

Morgana gave her a knowing smile and shook her head. "He's not coming."

"What did you do to Eli?" She wasn't just scared anymore. She was angry.

If this bitch hurt Eli I'm going to kill her.

"Ulrik! Ulrik!" She scooted back across the floor. One of them would would hear and come help her.

"He's not going to hear you either." Morgana's statement held such a note of triumphant satisfaction Willow felt her stomach drop. Dread clawed at her insides.

She already knew the answer, but she asked anyway. "Why?"

"He's dead." Morgana's maniacal smile chilled her to the bone.

In that moment she thought of Anippe and what Ulrik had been planning. Did that mean Eli was dead too? She willed the tears away as her body shook with fury. Right now she preferred the anger and rage that was coursing through her veins to the bottomless pit of despair that she wanted to disappear into if Eli was in fact dead.

If only Morgana didn't have Mathilda she could try and fight her and hope that Phaedra or Gamal, someone, anyone would find them soon.

"Why did you have to kill him?" She managed to say through clenched teeth.

"Just another thing that Killian will thank me for. Ulrik's been on his shit list ever since he disappeared. Plus, he'd become suspicious of me in Greece. Constantly sniffing around. First with Mathilda..."

"What? What about Mathilda?" Willow looked at the young girl who was frightened and penned to the wall."

"Oh." Morgana looked amused. "Well I just have to tell someone this story because it's just too good. That morning of Mathilda and Zoriana's big blow up in the woods, I'd left to go "gather" materials for a spell." She put air quotes around the word gather. "I'd really headed out so I could report back to Killian, but then Mathilda who'd been running away from her fight with mommy caught me communicating with him. You see with magic, I'd been able to devise a way to talk to Killian without him being able to detect our location so he couldn't try and get around me without giving me what he promised." Morgana was so pleased with herself. Willow was waiting on her to physically pat herself on the back for a job well done.

"Anyways, what was I saying? Oh yeah, Mathilda... I couldn't let her go running back to camp and rat me out, so I put her to sleep. Since she was already fighting with Mommy Dearest it made it easy to keep their feud going without too many questions being asked. Good thing I already had a forget potion on hand. A good healthy dose of that would have lasted a while before I had to give her another. Then I brewed a potion that would keep her angry and alienated from the person she cared about most in this world."

Willow noticed something flicker in Morgana's eyes when she referenced Mathilda and Zoriana's close relationship. Was it envy or jealousy she saw? She wasn't sure. Eli had said Morgana was an orphan. Had she known her mother at all?

"Administered every few days, it kept her right where I wanted her: by my side where I could keep a constant watch on her to make sure the potion wouldn't wear off without anyone being the wiser. It's natural after a horrible fight with her mom she would seek solace with me, her makeshift big sister. This way she couldn't go running and spilling her guts." Hopefully, the longer Morgana spent sharing her plans the quicker someone would find them. When she chanced a quick glance at Max, she saw the shallow breaths that made his chest rise and fall. Good. He was hanging on despite the silver that was burning his skin and poisoning his blood.

"The other day when Ulrik asked her about her eyes, I knew he recognized the potion from the effects it has on you after you've drank it. It was only a matter of time before he divulged what he suspected. Just happened to work out that we would find the book before he could actually get around to telling on me." Morgana was like a cat with a bowl of cream she was so ecstatic over her plans coming together.

"That's why I tried to kill him on the battlefield, but wasn't able to finish the job because I had to take care of Katana. She was going to ruin everything. Once I sent her and the other vampires on the way, the sooner I could find this book that meant so much to Killian and he'd reward me with what I wanted. If Katana got you or the book before I did, the deal was off the table. I couldn't have that."

A chill ran down her spine at Morgana's words, she was so cool and calculating. Her mind still couldn't fathom that for years she'd played this role and fooled them all, but why? Why did she wait so long?

"I just don't understand why you did any of this. Why did you betray us?" It was hard to keep the hurt from showing.

There was no remorse or sorrow when she stared into Morgana's eyes. "Story for another time. You'll know all my reasons soon enough. Now give me the book."

"I can't do that."

Morgana's answer was to use her magic to choke Mathilda. With her arms still penned to the wall, she couldn't clutch at her throat like most people would when they were choking. Her body twitched and spasmed trying desperately to fill her lungs with oxygen. Drool ran down the side of her mouth. A tear fell down Willow's face as she watched the girl's eyes roll into the back of her head.

"Okay. Stop." She let out a breath. Her shoulders slumped. "I'll give you the book. Just please stop hurting her." Willow awkwardly scrambled to her feet, maintaining her hold on the book. Morgana's smile pissed her off.

"And since there's no one here to stop me I'll take you and the book to Killian."

The smug expression taunted Willow. Why wasn't there something she could do? She felt so helpless. If she tried to fight, Morgana might kill one or both of them. She couldn't take that risk.

"Fine." The defeat she felt carved out her insides. "Let them go and you can take me."

Morgana eyed her. "Not both of them."

"You said you wouldn't hurt either of them."

"Yes, but I didn't say I would let them both out of their traps. Once you get over here and hand me the book, then I'll let Mathilda go. She can help Max once we're gone."

Damn it. Why does she have to be so smart?

She was thinking of everything. Guess you didn't get to be an evil genius if you didn't think ten steps ahead of everyone else. "As soon as I hand you the book, you let her down."

"Yeah, we agreed on this already. Let's go before one of the others finds us." Impatience seeped into her tone.

Willow's steps dragged as she walked the distance to Morgana. Her eyes went to Mathilda's face and she offered up a silent apology to the girl that she couldn't have done more.

"Don't Willow." Max's weak plea made her want to cry.

"I don't have a choice. I won't let you guys get killed because of me." A sob choked her when she reached Morgana. "Let her go."

"Book first."

She had no more leverage, no more cards to play, nothing up her sleeve. With deep reluctance and regret she handed Morgana the book. She hadn't expected her to keep her word but Mathilda fell to the ground the minute she relinquished the book. Morgana was about to grab her so they could teleport out of the tomb when Morgana cried out and stumbled to the side. Blood stained her shirt on the side.

"Run Willow!"

Willow took a few steps back from Morgana. "I'm not leaving without you guys." She called to Mathilda. Voices could be heard coming from the entrance. Morgana recovered quickly from the injury Mathilda inflicted. She heard the voices too.

What happened next seemed to occur in slow motion and sped up all at once. There was no way she could have stopped Morgana and then she disappeared, taking The Book of Prophecy with her.

CHAPTER 22

Eli

BLURRY VISION WASN'T the only side effect he had from being knocked unconscious. His head hurt and he had ringing in his ears. It took a second for him to remember where he was.

Valley of the Kings.

Once everything flooded his mind, he rushed to his feet and swayed from getting up too fast.

How long was I knocked out?

He wasn't in complete and utter darkness. His flashlight lay on the floor of the tomb a few feet away. The beam cast an eerie shadow on the wall. As he dusted himself off, he realized it had to be Ulrik that bashed him over the head. He seethed with anger for trusting the son of a bitch.

The thought occurred to him that Ulrik could have gone after Morgana before or after he dispatched with him. Fear shot through him. "Morgana." He knew he shouldn't call out. What if Ulrik was still here? Something told him Ulrik was smart enough to flee the scene of the crime and not hang around. He grabbed his flashlight and started shining it about to see if he saw her body laying anywhere.

Alarm bells were going off. He could have taken Morgana hostage and went looking for Willow. He knew he had to find Morgana first before he could go racing from the tomb to find Willow, but he was anxious, nervous and scared. If Ulrik got to Willow there might not be any saving her.

"Morgana." He shined the light frantically around the tomb. Then the shaft of light landed on something. Something was off as he approached. The body was nearly perfectly mummified and looked like it should have been entombed in the sarcophagus that sat behind the glass. There was something familiar about the body. He nearly dropped the flashlight as recognition dawned.

The corpse was Ulrik. Someone had used magic to drain every drop of blood from his body. That meant one of two things, Morgana was safe and had gained the upper hand on him and fled or... the alternative made his blood run cold. He went tearing towards the entrance of the tomb. He had to find the others. Hopefully, it wasn't too late.

When he exited the tomb he realized he didn't remember which one he'd seen them run into. He ran to the nearest one and called out as he shined his flashlight. At this point, he didn't care if the noise he made alerted security. He wanted to find everyone.

His heart wouldn't stop racing. He decided they weren't in the tomb he'd entered and rushed from it and went to the next one. This tomb was well lit. Maybe they were in this one. He was about to call out when he heard a woman's loud wail.

"Willow" He bellowed and raced into the tomb unsure what he would find.

His heart was in his throat as he panicked over what he would find below. He skidded to a halt when he came into the chamber. The first person he laid eyes on was Willow. Their eyes met across the distance. He wanted to breathe a huge sigh of relief, but when he heard the loud wail again, he was pulled from her gaze. What he saw made him feel like someone had kicked him in the chest and left a big gaping hole.

For a minute, it didn't even register that he was walking, but then his brain was back in his body and he moved slow and stiff towards the scene on the floor. He hoped his eyes were playing tricks on him. When he reached them, he dropped to his knees and took her hand.

Zoriana's face was buried in the hair of her lifeless daughter. Mathilda's eyes were still open. They stared blankly up at the ceiling. Blood ran from her nose and her ears. He was stunned. He couldn't stop staring. That wasn't Mathilda. Tears stood in his eyes when he looked up at Willow with his mouth hung open in a question. She had her arms wrapped around herself. Her body shook with the force of her weeping.

When he was finally able to tear his eyes away he looked over and saw off to the side that Phaedra cradled Max in her arms. Was he dead too or just unconscious? Tears spilled from her eyes. In all the years they'd known each other, he'd never seen her cry before.

Who did this?

The question sat on the tip of his tongue, but he was too scared to ask and hear the answer. He couldn't get the horrible, guttural sounds of Zoriana's cries out of his head. She'd just lost her only child. He didn't know how to comfort her.

A loud cry tore through the air. It was seconds before he realized it had come from him. He cried out again, trying to release the physical pain that sat heavy in his gut at losing Mathilda. His head fell into his hands and then he felt Willow's hands on his shoulders and around him. He leaned back into her.

His eyes returned to Mathilda once more. He wanted to tell his little cousin to get up, but he knew she wouldn't.

"Sana! Sana!" Zoriana repeated frantically, the white light glowing from beneath her hands, but having no effect.

How long had she tried to resurrect her daughter, despite knowing their magic was incapable of that.

"My baby!" Zoriana sobbed and howled. The hurt he felt intensified at what he imagined Zoriana was feeling after losing a daughter she'd never had the opportunity to get things right with. The two had never settled whatever it was between them and now they never would.

All he could think about was the teenage girl who was eager to talk about spells and magic potions and who probably hadn't had her first kiss yet. Now she would never have any of that again.

He finally found the breath to ask the question he didn't want the answer to. "Who... who did this?"

Willow's tears fell on his neck. "Mor..." It was a struggle for her to say the name, like the name was getting caught on something as it tried to exit her throat. "Morgana... she killed her and took The Book of Prophecy." She rushed out the last part.

The betrayal sat like bile in the back of his throat. Even if he could have spewed it up at that moment, the poison of it would still be running through his veins much like the silver ran through Max's veins. How long had she been plotting and scheming to betray them? She'd known Mathilda since she was born. How could she so easily kill her? All of these thoughts plagued his head and his heart.

CHAPTER 23

Willow

MORGANA HAD BEEN like a hurricane leaving devastation and destruction in her wake. The aftermath had been brutal and was still causing Willow physical pains. The loss of both Mathilda and Ulrik was too hard to put into words. The last few mornings she'd woken up with Zoriana's ragged cries still reverberating in her head and the soul-crushing grief on poor Anippe's face when they told her Ulrik was killed still haunted her.

They hadn't left Egypt yet because there was an issue with transporting Mathilda's body out of the country since she had been murdered.

Alistair teleported in the next morning after it happened. Zoriana was inconsolable. They were mostly keeping her sedated because she would sleep and then wake up and have these screaming fits when she realized

Mathilda was no longer alive. She was like an open wound that just wouldn't heal. Every morning the scab got violently ripped off. It was one of the most painful things she'd ever had to watch.

Everything was just different. She felt different. Morgana's betrayal blindsided them and was already a tough pill to swallow on its own, but her murdering Mathilda gutted them. She felt like someone had hollowed out her insides. They were all walking around in a daze.

Max was still recovering from the silver poisoning. The supernatural doctor that cared for him said if the bullet had been just a few inches closer to the heart, he wouldn't have survived.

She had yet to tell everyone all the vile things Morgana shared with her. There would be time enough for that.

All she'd been able to think about was how selfless Mathilda had been. The instant Morgana released her, the first thing she did was try and keep Morgana from taking her. She hadn't considered her own life for a second. Of course she was sure that none of them thought Morgana would kill anyone. Now there were two dead bodies and a trail of bleeding, broken hearts. Everyone was dealing with their grief in their own way. Phaedra and Eli had taken to sparring every day. He usually came back with fresh bruises or blood. She was sure Phaedra wore matching bruises and injuries. Even when they made love now it was like they were trying to fuck the pain away. Sometimes it bordered on painful, but she needed it, she needed him. She hadn't felt a loss like this since her mother and knew there was so much she was suppressing, anything to keep her from feeling. Helping Gamal and Anippe make funeral arrangements for Ulrik kept her busy. She'd gone back and forth over whether to tell Anippe about the conversation she'd had with Ulrik before he was killed. Eventually she did. It was important she know that Ulrik intended to love her despite all the ugliness that threatened them. The news broke the girl's heart even further. She let Anippe cry on her shoulder despite the fact they didn't know each other that well. At least she now knew that Ulrik had been determined not to give up on them again.

It was good to be useful to everyone, which helped her suppress the grieving and sadness to welcome the hate that now grew in her heart for Killian and Morgana. It had taken root and grown like a vine, twisted and snarling and wrapping itself around her heart. She would use the hatred as fuel to feed her when she felt like quitting. She was going to spend day and night mastering her Oracle and fae abilities, and then, she was going to hunt down Killian and Morgana and kill them both.

To Be Continued

***

Continue The Oracle Chronicles Series in the next novel,
Empowered.
www.moniboyce.com/series/oraclechronicles/

Keep up with Moni's releases by joining her newsletter!
www.moniboyce.com

Also By Moni Boyce:
Redemption of the Heart

MONI BOYCE

NON-ENGLISH WORDS & PHRASES USED

LATIN

Reperio – discover

Indica mihi quem quaerimus – Show me that which we seek.

Terra ortum – earth rise

Amplificio – amplify

Maiorum, audierit a senioribus. Est autem repleti sunt ut indignus te et potestatem spirituum. Auferte hereditate sua tacere et audire non possunt vocibus et industria. - Ancestors, hear the elders. There is one unworthy to be filled with your spirits and power. Remove his heritage, his birthright and silence your voices and energy so he may hear them no more.

Integumentum – shield, protect

GREEK

Párte tis tsántes tous tóra. - Take their bags now.

Geia sas – hello

DANISH

Hej – hello

Møgkælling – bitch

Fanden – shit

ARABIC

Ma aldhy tafealuh huna – What are you doing here?

ACKNOWLEDGMENTS

First and foremost, I want to thank God, because without him none of this would be possible. I'm grateful to have the time and means to do something I love and I love storytelling.

I want to acknowledge and thank my family and friends for always supporting and encouraging me. My parents and my sisters are some of the best hype men I could ever ask for. It means a lot to have them in my corner.

Again, I just want to send a huge shout out to Mallory Rock who designed the covers for the series because she did a phenomenal job.

A really big thank you and shout out to all of my readers. You guys rock for buying and reading this book. I hope you enjoyed it enough to buy and read the next book in the series. I know there are lots of ways you could spend your money and your time and it means a lot that you chose to spend it reading my book. You have my gratitude.

What Did You Think of Enlightened: The Oracle Chronicles?

First of all, thank you for purchasing this book **Enlightened: The Oracle Chronicles**. *I know you could have picked any number of books to read, but you picked this book and for that I am extremely grateful.*

I hope that it added value and quality to your everyday life. If so, it would be really nice if you could share this book with your friends and family by posting to Facebook and Twitter.

If you enjoyed this book and found some benefit in reading this, I'd like to hear from you and hope that you could take some time to post a review. Your feedback and support will help me as an author to greatly improve my writing craft for future projects and make this book even better.

I want you, the reader, to know that your review is very important and so, if you'd like to **leave a review**, *all you have to do is go to Amazon, Goodreads or Bookbub. I wish you all the best in your future success!*

About the Author

Moni Boyce is a writer, filmmaker, poet and author of contemporary and paranormal romance. She spent the last fifteen years working in the film industry and now creates characters of her own and brings them to life on the page. Moni has ghostwritten romance novellas and novels for over a year now and decided to put some of her own creations out in the world. She considers herself a bookworm, film buff, foodie, music lover and an avid world traveler having visited 33 countries and counting. She lives a bit of a nomadic life, but considers Los Angeles home. Which is the subject of her first travel book: Greater Than A Tourist – Los Angeles, California: 50 Travel Tips From A Local. Learn more about her at www.moniboyce.com

http://www.facebook.com/MoniBoyceWrites
http://www.amazon.com/author/moniboyce
http://www.twitter.com/MoniBoyce
http://www.bookbub.com/authors/moni-boyce
http://www.goodreads.com/moniboyce